I0831214

March of the Phantoms

A novel

Translated from French

H. Erdal YALT

Editor

Cleo Hanlon Liebl

ISBN 978-0-578-18817-1

Lulu Enterprises, Inc.
3101 Hillsborough St.
Raleigh, NC 27607
USA

Cover painting:

"Fading Footsteps"

1984

acrylic on canvas 36"X48"

from Uprooted series

by

Lucy Janjigian

Printed in the

United States of America

www.lulu.com
2016

Preface

Hayri is a low level clerk at the Turkish consulate to France, a position he loves because he can polish his French accent and wander the streets of the city he loves. However, he drank a bit too much at the reception and decided to hop a ride home in the ambassador's limo. He should have walked home. The Phantom is a brief glimpse into a young man's everyday life in Paris, his mother, his fellow consulate worker, a German woman, a Turkish girl, and the 'thing' that is following him, stalking him in his dreams, leaking into his waking hours. And the Indian psychiatrist who's helping him chase the Phantom.

Bring your EuroPass for this tale though cultures and Phantoms.

Cleo Hanlon Liebl

This is a work of fiction. Names, characters, places and incidents are the product of the author's imagination or are used fictitiously. Any resemblance to actual events, locales, or persons, living or dead, is entirely coincidental.

Phantom: something apparent to sense but with no substantial existence.
(www.merriam-webster.com/dictionary/phantom)

I

Better the sleepless night, then the nightmare.

Accidents happen

The floor nurse, cutting short her conversation on the phone, turned to the police officer who was waiting:

“What is the patient's name, officer?”

The young policeman, handsome in his uniform, fixed the blue eyes of the beautiful woman. He smiled and stepped closer, leaning over to show her the paper he was holding in his hand.

“I do not know how to pronounce his name,” he said.

The nurse, accustomed to flirtatious patients, took a step back. After a quick glance at the paper, she smiled:

“Ah! This is the Turkish gentleman of room 310. He has a name rather difficult to pronounce: Hay-ret-tine Al-per-gune.”

The young officer tried to repeat:

“Hay....”

She indicated the corridor:

“Fifth door on the right.”

It was visiting hours and hospital corridors were crowded with busy people. They all looked sullen, unlike those usually seen outside, in the streets of Paris. After all, they were in a hospital.

Being careful not to disturb the visitors, the officer walked slowly, checking the numbers on the doors.

Suddenly a horrible roar nailed everyone in his place. By reflex, the right hand of the officer touched the hilt of his gun. He quickened his walk in the direction where all heads were turned to. He stopped in front of a door where some curious visitors were trying to understand what was happening.

In an authoritative tone, he told them to step back. The hand still on the hilt of his gun, ready to draw if necessary, he walked over and read the number on the door ajar:

“Three hundred and ten.”

A lady passed him hustling and rushed into the room. She shouted:

“Hayri! Oğlum[1]”

The officer had no time to react. He screamed after her:

“Stop madam!”

His order had no effect on the lady. Fallowing her, he entered room with cautious steps. He has got surprised by what he saw.

The lady was near the bed, holding the head of a man. She should be in her sixties. The man in the bed seemed in his thirties.

He looked at the officer with an embarrassed smile.

“Ah! Officer,” he said. “I'm sorry. I was dreaming. Well.., I was having a nightmare.”

So, all this noise was nothing but a nightmare. A second woman was standing in the middle of the room with a broom in hand. She was younger. Having seen the police, she talked to the man in bed:

“You see, my Monsieur? This time your screams bring the police.”

She had a strong Portuguese accent and her smile was betraying the irony.

“I am really sorry officer,” repeated the man in the bed. “I'm not totally out of the effects of the accident yet.”

The young policeman finally calmed down and pulled his hand from the hilt of his gun.

“Are you Mr. Al-per ...?”

“Yes, I'm Hayrettin Alpergun. But they often call me Hayri. How can I help you, officer?”

---

[1] My son! (Turkish)

The policeman took out a folder from his bag.

“I brought your typed deposition of the accident. Would you read it and sign please?”

“Ah yes, grumbled Hayri. It needs to be signed, right?”

He seemed annoyed. The officer noticed his hesitation.

“Do you want to change your deposition, monsieur?”

“No, no! Not at all! Replied Hayri.”

Then he spoke in Turkish to the woman near his bedside:

“I want all to be over, mom. I want to forget this accident, the formalities and the deposition to the police, everything…”

“And the nightmares too,” she added in French.

Hayri looked back at the officer with a forced smile:

“You see? Ever since I had this accident, the nightmares don’t leave me alone.”

“An inspector from The Security Department will come to your visit this afternoon, to ask a few questions,” said the policeman.

Noticing Hayri’s nervousness, he felt obliged to explain:

“As you have a diplomatic status, the Department has decided to launch a small investigation. The inspector will come just for a couple of questions.”

“Ah! Procedures,” said Hayri with a forced smile. So there would be an investigation.

"All those formalities for a stupid accident?" thought Hayri. But he wasn't the one who was driving, at the time of the accident. He was at the back seat.

He looked at the paper held to him, and tried to concentrate on reading.

> *The cocktail party at the exhibition hall was still going on. But Madam Consul told me that I could go. It suited me because I was not at all interested in modern painting.*
>
> *I should first go through the Street of Ankara to get today's mail at the Embassy, then I would be free.*
>
> *Leaving the building, I met Ahmet, one of our drivers. He said he would take the official car of Madam Consul at the Embassy, and could give me a ride.*
>
> *Although our office is in the building of the OECD, as a rule, official cars with ordinary Parisian plates, must be returned before the night to the garage of the Embassy.*
>
> *Apparently, Madam Consul had plans for the end of the afternoon, other than returning to work.*

"Did I really say that?" thought Hayri.

> *The seat next to the driver was cluttered with files. So, I settled into the back seat. The radio was playing an old Italian song:*
>
> > *Lasciatemi cantare, una canzone piano piano ...*
>
> *Obviously Ahmet, the driver, was taking advantage of the absence of the Madam Consul.*

Hayri stopped reading for a moment. His eyes turned to the window to watch the gray sky of Paris. He thought:

"Did I really told all this to the police, after the accident? I must have drunk too many daiquiris. This is perhaps why the Madam Consul asked me to leave earlier than scheduled."

He cast a glance at the officer who was observing him with curiosity and returned to his reading.

> *I think we were driving at high speed...*

It came to his mind the accident that claimed the life of Princess Diana and could not keep his lips to contract in a bitter smile, avoiding the gaze of the police.

> *But I'm sure we were below the limit.*

Ah! He had to save the driver, right? Did Ahmet drink, too?

> *I was flipping through the Turkish newspapers left on the back seat. All dated from the day before.*
>
> *It all happened in a second. I first felt the sudden braking and heard Ahmet's swearing:*
>
> *"Ha siquetir[2]!"*

Did he say that too? Fortunately it was typed with French spelling. It was funny.

> *Then we hit a shadow. I mean a man.*

But those guys, they had typed word by word all what he told them.

[2] F.. off!

Then the car made a spin, tilting a little to the right. For a moment, I felt that we were going to collide with the bus traveling in the opposite direction. At this point our vehicle struck one of the cars parked along the curb and stopped. The man we hit remained a second on the hood, his face pressed to the windshield, then slipped between two cars.

At this point, he stopped again. He had deliberately omitted one detail. Despite the shock, he had clearly seen man's horrified large black eyes. Eyes deeply sunken, staring inside the car like he was trying to see something. Although Hayri had been too talkative on other details, he had instinctively kept this one out of his deposition. It would be a useless information, anyway. He had learned in his political science education that any wise man should avoid giving unnecessary information to state officials, especially to the police. Because such information could provoke an unhealthy curiosity that could create complications later.

Stunned by the shock, I remained motionless. I saw the driver exiting the car. He open the left door to help me get out. But I could not make any movement. A neck pain prevented me from moving. The idea of being paralyzed has haunted me for a few moments.

Hayri touched the brace on his neck. He slowly turned his head left and right. It was not too bad.

"Good news," he said, and went back to reading.

Then the police and the ambulance have arrived. They took me out of the car.

October 11, 20...

This was the last line. The police had probably recorded all his remarks on tape. Otherwise, how could they transcribe all this nonsense without missing a single word?

The man they had hit, came to his mind. He was laying between the cars. The rescuers had difficulties reaching him. The alarm of the car parked in the curb was still screaming.

While they put a brace around his neck, they put an oxygen mask to the other man. The police helped the ambulance team to load him as quickly as possible in their vehicle. They left immediately.

But with Hayri, the same police did not rush. They asked questions about the accident. The idea to tell them that he has diplomatic immunity did not come to mind. Ahmet the driver was not in sight. Probably, they were questioning him too, but Hayri could not turn his head to look around.

He signed and returned the papers to the police, then asked:

"Do you know the identity of the man?"

The policeman, well trained, answered with poker face:

"Mr. Inspector will give you all the necessary details."

He wished him a quick recovery, greeted his mother politely and left.

Mrs. Alpergun noticed that her son was nervous. She spoke in French, again:

"But darling, you have a sore neck. Please stop touching your neck brace!"

Ever since Hayri had divorced and moved in with his mother, he was treated like a kid.

"Mom, leave me alone, please! Go smoke another cigarette!"

With these words, Mrs. Alpergun seemed taken aback.

"Well then, I am going to the cafeteria," she said coldly and left the room. The Portuguese servant left too.

His mother would probably complain later. "I am going to have to make my apologies," thought Hayri. But at that moment, he needed to be alone. He was holding up since his divorce and the death of his daughter. At least he was trying. But this stupid accident had change everything.

Left alone in the room, he thought of his daughter. He tried to cry, but failed again.

"No tear," he murmured. "Not a single one. Am I not unhappy? Ah, yes! But boys don't cry, isn't that right?"

He looked around. There was nobody in the room to hear him whispering like that but he still decided to keep quiet. His mouth closed immediately but his brain rebelled against this decision. How to get away from all these thoughts that make him even more miserable?

He wanted to get up. Two days in hospital and he had enough. Especially of this smell that exists in all the hospitals, this smell that makes you even sicker and almost vomit.

When he searched for the catheter planted on the back of his hand, he found nothing. He remembered that the nurse had taken it out that morning. It was no longer needed. Finally 'unchained', he smiled with satisfaction.

Could he also break the chains of his thoughts: his bad memories that made him sick at heart? The memories that caused him perhaps these nightmares since the accident?

But why a stupid accident would trigger a series of nightmares? Nightmares, after all, aren't they just dreams, bad dreams? But the ones that he was having now, did not look at all like those he had when he was a child. The ones that followed the assassination of his father!

“Ah! This smell is killing me!” he whispered.

He looked for his slippers. Where could they be? He must have left them on the other side of the bed.

“Who cares?” he said. “I go barefoot!”

As soon as his feet touched the cold floor tiles, he felt happy like a child. Among his friends, he had always admired those who had the courage of breaking the rules. This is what he would do now: break the rule. If his mom saw him like that, she would go mad.

He approached the window. But his hopes for the beautiful Parisian landscape vanished suddenly. The sky was hazy. Only the hospital's parking lot and the roofs of some houses were visible. In the distance, he vaguely distinguished the Montparnasse tower that stood like a phantom.

At the creak of the door, he tried in vain to turn his head but his brace stopped him. Was it his mother? Normally, she would not come back before half an hour. When he managed to turn with his whole body, he saw Sinan Bey pushing the door ajar.

“How are you doing with the nightmares, mon cher?” he said.

Sinan Bey liked to say 'mon cher[3]' in French to everyone and he believed that all the diplomats of the world said 'mon cher' when they talked among themselves. This was his way of having fun of them.

"Ah! Hello Sinan Bey."

Sinan Bey walked in and closed the door behind him. By putting his finger on his lips, he called Hayri to be silent. He walked to the bed and looked underneath. Then examined the closet, opened the door and inspected the inside.

"But, what are doing?" asked Hayri.

Sinan Bey and Hayri were old acquaintances. They both had studied at the same University in Ankara. Sinan Bey was three years older and was known among his friends for some strange behaviors. Since he was the oldest in the class, everybody called him with the title 'Bey[4]' and rumored he was a government agent.

He answered in a low voice.

"I am checking if there are any bugs."

Sinan Bey was working at the Turkish Embassy, located at the Street of Ankara. He said he was responsible for commercial affairs but Hayri knew he had a totally different mission.

"Bugs? In a hospital room?" asked Hayri, trying to give himself an angry look. He knew though what he meant by 'bugs'.

---

[3] Mon cher (Fr): My dear (friend).

[4] Bey (Turkish): Mister, Sir.

“As a diplomat of first class, mon cher, you should know that there can always be someone who could spy on you,” said Sinan Bey.

“You're not going to find anything here,” replied Hayri. And I'm far from being a ‘first class’ diplomat. Why on earth would anyone want to spy on me?

“Do not be modest, mon cher. You never know.”

He spoke slowly and took his time with each word. While speaking, he carefully examined Hayri’s face, as if trying to read his thoughts.

But Hayri was never able to speak slowly.

“Have you by any chance met my mother in the hallway?”

“How else would I know of your nightmares?”

Sinan Bey always liked to give answers in question form.

“You never know,” he said. “Could that be a ‘little bird’ whispering into your ear? Are you not always aware of everything that is happening everywhere?”

A brief smile appeared on the face of Sinan Bey.

“As a matter of fact, I talked to Mrs. Alpergun. She seemed worried about your condition.”

“My condition? Do you know that my mother likes to be worried about everything? All kind of worries have always been her favorite occupation.”

Surprised by this response, Sinan Bey’s smile faded. He took a serious look.

“The ambassador asked me to launch an investigation for this accident.”

"What!?"

The two men looked at each other for a few seconds in silence. Sinan Bey replied with a calm voice:

"The man you crashed is still in a coma."

Sinan Bey's strange looks were starting to be annoying.

"But we did not crash," said Hayri. "We just touched him, a little."

"You mean 'touché', like in the swordplay?"

Was there some sarcasm in his voice?

"But Sinan Bey, you know that I was at the back seat. This was Madam Consul's driver Ahmet who was driving the car. I think it was one of the armored cars of the Embassy."

"Ah! So, it was one of the cars of the Embassy?"

"Yes."

"Armored?"

Hayri did not answer. It was obvious now his friend was having fun of him. With Sinan Bey, one never knew if he was serious or not.

A few more seconds passed in silence before Sinan Bey started to talk again. This time he looked really serious.

"Have you noticed that the car did not have a plate of the diplomatic corps, but an ordinary car license Parisian?"

Hayri was well aware of this makeup. The term 'CD[5]' put on the car created sometimes more problems than a regular car. Especially when one is trying to avoid reporters.

"Yes. So what?" he said.

"The police is always put on alert in accidents involving diplomatic or VIP cars."

"Is that so?"

"Especially, if the accident is rather bizarre."

"Bizarre!? You think the accident was 'bizarre'?" asked Hayri.

Sinan Bey finally smiled.

"What I think mon cher, is no matter. What matters now, is what the French police think."

"Ah, the French!" said Hayri with visible anger. "They are always the same. They will let the camels pass, but stop the ants."

Sinan Bey's face became more serious than ever.

"You mock with the French later. By the way, aren't you supposed to be lying in bed?"

Hayri took these words as an order and obeyed. Moreover, he felt tired.

Once in bed, he asked:

"I think you are holding your tongue, Sinan Bey. Would you explain to me clearly what is happening, please?"

---

[5] CD: Corps Diplomatique.

Sinan Bey was able to play with his facial expressions as he wanted. Hayri had learned that during his university years when he met him in Ankara.

His smile became a little bitter this time and said:

“If a person deliberately throws himself before a moving car mon cher, it's called a suicide attempt.”

This time Hayri understood. This was the reason why the accident was rated as ‘bizarre’. The man, who was in coma now, had then tried to kill himself by jumping in the path of the car.

“Are you sure? Is that what police told you?”

“You're naive, mon cher. The police would never tell you such things. They show us a poker face. Remember our college years. I was and I still am, a good poker player. When I spoke to the Inspector of the Police on the phone, I immediately felt there was something fishy in this case. So, I did make my little investigation. I spoke to a Turkish grocer around the corner. He had spotted an old lady, talking to the police, witness to the accident. Then I found that lady, pretending to be a journalist. She was very happy to tell me what she saw. It was she who uttered the word ‘suicide’ when talking to the police.”

“So this is a story of old woman,” said Hayri

The door opened and Mrs. Alpergun entered.

“Is there any news, Sinan Bey?” she asked curiously.

She certainly had listened at the door and probably heard everything. With her appearance, Sinan Bey changed the tone of his voice:

"Nothing more than what I already told you, madam," he answered respectfully.

"Do they know the identity of the man? I just heard in the cafeteria that he is still in a coma."

Hayri smiled. Apparently, his mom was making her own investigation. Sinan Bey continued:

"Based on the information that was given to me this morning, the police has not found yet his identity but the inspector that I had on the phone, told me that the victim of the accident could be an immigrant from a Middle Eastern country. He can be Arab, Iranian, Palestinian or even Turkish. How unfortunate coincidence that Hayri and he were rushed to the same hospital. I see that this makes my friend a little nervous."

"You're right Sinan Bey," she said. "This is why my son has nightmares. You'll see, as soon he is back home, there will be no more nightmares. This is the hospital that makes him sick."

"Stop your nonsense, Mom!" exclaimed Hayri.

Somehow, he agreed that once away from this hospital smell, he would feel much better.

His mother was curious and Sinan Bey was more generous with her in giving information. She took the opportunity to ask more questions:

"Didn't he have any ID on him? He is in the hospital for almost two days. Nobody came to search for him? Was he living alone?"

"He may be an illegal immigrant," said Sinan Bey.

Hayri and his mother looked at him with curiosity. Sinan Bey, thinking he already said too much, changed the subject.

“Okay, now I must go. I'll pass by later this afternoon or tomorrow morning. You will give me the details of the conversation with the inspector,” he said to Hayri.

Hayri felt tired and wanted to be alone. An idea came to his mind.

“Sinan Bey, did you come with your car?”

“Yes, why?”

“Would you please take my mother home? She has been in the hospital with me since the accident and she is very tired.”

Mrs. Alpergun prepared to refuse, but the voice of Sinan Bey was authoritative.

“Hayri is right, ma'am. You look tired. So, I'll drive you home. Once released from the hospital, Hayri will still need you. So, you must rest.

This was reasonable. She accepted.

***

He woke up screaming.

This time nobody rushed into the room. People at the hospital had probably got used to his screams.

His heart was beating so hard that he thought for a moment of having heart attack. He had sweated. His shirt was soaked. He put himself in sitting position and tried to calm down.

A few minutes later, a nurse walked in with a tray of drugs. Hayri checked his watch. The visiting time had already passed.

"You were sleeping a while ago," said the nurse. "So I did not want to disturb, but when I heard you..."

"Screaming?" said Hayri, trying to smile.

She smiled back.

"It's time for your medicine, monsieur. I will also check your brace."

She approached the bed.

"Forgive my curiosity, but in your nightmares, what makes you so terrified, monsieur?"

Obviously the rumor was quickly dispersing within the hospital. He found the question rather amusing. But would he really tell her everything?

After the death of his daughter, he wanted to flee from Turkey. All he needed was a change. A mission abroad would be nice. So now he was in Paris, again…

This accident had happened about a month after his arrival. Although he was bored in that bed, he knew that a few days of 'forced vacation' would not hurt. After all, here, he had all the luxury of a five star hotel.

So, he decided to satisfy the curiosity of the nurse.

"I'll tell you. But first, could you change my shirt please?"

"Of course monsieur," she said, going to the closet.

She returned with a new shirt. But first, she had to remove the brace that Hayri had decided to give a different name: the ‘necklace’.

“There's something behind me,” he said.

The nurse, focused on changing the shirt, leaned over to see what he had on his back. There was nothing. She moved the pillow to see if there was something behind.

“But I see nothing, monsieur.”

Hayri laughed.

“In my nightmares, madam,” he said. “It is in my nightmares that this ‘thing’ appears, right behind me.”

The nurse looked at him stupidly.

When he was a child, his father was murdered in an ambush. And then, decades later, a few months ago, his little daughter Seray had died of leukemia. Hayri had all the reasons to have nightmares. But the nightmares were not introduced until this stupid accident. He had to explain it all to the nurse, but how?

“These last two days, I mean since I am in this hospital, I can’t have a good sleep, ma'am.”

She looked offended.

“But this is of the best hospitals in France, monsieur.”

“No doubt ma'am. My nightmares have nothing to do with your hospital. I recently lost my little daughter of leukemia, she was only five years old. I was very unhappy. A month ago, I registered myself to an international mission to Paris. I brought my mother with me. Everything was going well until the accident.

She was still looking at him with curiosity. Hayri wanted to have some fun by exaggerating a little the story.

“There's something out there waiting for me in the abstract world. This ‘thing’ expects me to fall asleep. Then it begins to follow me. I want to run but I can’t. My legs get so heavy that I can’t move.”

“What is this thing, monsieur? A monster? A fierce animal?”

Hayri showed his ‘necklace’.

“I do not know ma'am. I can’t turn my head to look back.”

The nurse finally realized that there was also a little joke in what the patient said.

“You must take this medicine before your meal, monsieur,” she said, in a dry voice.

Hayri swallowed the pill she handed.

A server entered with his meal. He arranged the service that allowed patients to eat without leaving the bed.

The doctor came in as the nurse and the server were leaving the room.

“How are you doing, today, Mr. Alpergun?”

He was a nice man with jovial face covered with a white beard. He had recently been in Turkey. This was not his first visit to this ‘land of dreams’ as he called. During his youth, he had traveled to eastern Anatolia.

“As you know, I'm afraid of sleeping,” replied Hayri.

“Tonight, we'll give you a sleeping pill and you'll be able to sleep without problem.”

‘Sleeping without problem!’ Does this mean that during his sleep, this ‘thing’ -whatever it is- would not bother him?

The doctor was reading his thoughts.

“This is a kind of sleeping pill that will prevent you having dreams. You will not need to run away your ‘pursuer’.”

There was a silence. The doctor seemed to wait for his patient tell something. Hayri decided to let his guard down and talk to him frankly.

“During my childhood, I lived in France with my family.”

“I know, said the doctor. You already told me. This is probably why you don’t have an accent.”

This was a compliment.

“My father was a civil servant at the Embassy. I learned French at school. My first days were difficult but I got quickly over it. My friends were nice to me.”

“Did you understand everything teachers were speaking in class?”

“Not everything. But I was making progress every day.”

Maybe it was the time to tell him about certain memories.

“One day when I was returning from school. I got off the bus and started walking toward the house. I saw in the distance an old woman with her dog.

They were walking towards me. Suddenly, the dog began to pull on his leash and the woman released the leash. The dog was huge. A mass of 'black wool' rushed towards me."

Hayri pretended not to notice the smile of doctor. Yes, he had always been afraid of dogs. So what?

He continued to tell his unfortunate encounter with the dog:

"My god, he was coming fast! I just had time to put my back to a wall and wait. He approached me. I was panicked. I pretended to throw my bag to threaten him. The dog stood back and started barking."

"If you did not make a gesture with your bag, he probably would have done nothing."

"Easy to say, said Hayri. I was a little boy and I never had a dog."

"Did he bite you?"

"No. But he tried. I was so scared. The old woman was finally near us. She was shouting: "*Stop Laika! Stop*!" But the dog did not obey her. Finally some people ran to my rescue. The old lady was very embarrassed. The dog would have taken me for the son of the family. That's why he had ran towards me."

The doctor no longer took the trouble to hide his smile. Hayri thought he talked too much.

"In your nightmares, is it a dog who is chasing you?" asked the doctor.

"No," responded Hayri with a sharp voice.

Would he tell him the rest of the story?

"A terrible news was waiting for me at home," he added.

It was too late to turn back. He continued:

"There were people at home. People I did not know... They said they were from the Embassy. My mother was lying on the couch, eyes closed. For a moment I thought she was dead."

He sighed for a moment. My God! It is difficult to talk about this, despite the years that had passed. The doctor was listening carefully.

"People from the Embassy told me that there had been a plot. Assassins had attacked the Embassy car, believing that the ambassador was inside. But the ambassador was not there. Instead my father was. They killed him."

He paused. He had a lump in his throat. The doctor came over and patted his shoulder:

"Do not be embarrassed to cry, my friend," he said.

"My problem, doctor, is that I can't cry!"

***

The shrill sound of a car alarm, screaming probably for nothing, woke him.

"Well, at least this time I did have not have a nightmare," he told himself.

The clock on the wall was indicating 7pm. By waking up, the annoying sound of the alarm had probably saved him from another nightmare.

He was hungry. Why did they not bring the dinner?

He remembered that he had asked a favor to the doctor. Tonight, he was authorized to walk to the cafeteria by himself.

"I'm free!" he said.

He was developing the habit of thinking aloud. This was not a good sign. He got off the bed barefoot. But where were the slippers? Of course, they were lying under the bed.

First, he went to the bathroom, washed his hands and face. His 'necklace' made it difficult. He looked at himself in the mirror and examined his tragicomic appearance. Wrinkles; did they increase? Does he have some grey in hair?

He tried to sing the *Jewel Song* from the Opera Faust:

> *Ah ! je ris de me voir si belle en ce miroir*[6]

But he had to give up quickly. A pain in the neck forced him to stop.

Once in the hallway, he felt happy like a child. He saw patients walking slowly, like a movie in slow motion. He walked slowly, too. He decided to enjoy every moment of his freedom. In a hospital, the minutes seemed longer than in the streets of Paris.

No nurse was in sight. There was nobody in the office of the floor nurse. He walked towards the elevator and pressed the call button.

After a minute of waiting, which seemed to him too long, another patient came. They said 'hi' to each other. Hayri looked at the level indicator above the elevator door. The cabin was frozen in the sixth. He turned his head

[6] Ah! I laugh to see myself so beautiful in this mirror

slowly towards the end of the hallway to read the sign ESCALIERS[7] in red letters on a door.

Undecided which path to take, he looked at the man who was near him. He was smiling.

The favorite topic to start a conversation in a hospital was always about a disease.

“I'm here for a prostate adenoma. It is a benign tumor that will not kill me,” the man said.

Hayri remained silent.

The man, keen to start a conversation, asked:

“What about you?”

Hayri replied showing his brace:

“I was given this necklace after a car accident.”

The man had an exaggerated laughter.

“I'm Gouteferd. François Gouteferd,” he said.

They shook hands.

“I'm Hayrettin Alpergun.”

The man made an effort to repeat. Hayri helped:

“You can call me Hayri.”

The elevator doors opened. They entered.

---

[7] Stairs

“I am teacher of physics at the high school,” said the man.

He pressed the button indicating CAFETERIA. The cabin shook.

“I'm in the Turkish delegation in OECD[8],” said Hayri.

Noticing that he was quoting the name of the organization in English, he corrected immediately for French:

“Uh!... I mean OCDE.”

He was sometimes forgetting that French were reading such acronyms in a different order: like OTAN (NATO), SIDA (AIDS), etc.

“You are a diplomat?” asked the man.

“Yes, I guess we can say that,” replied Hayri.

The elevator stopped and the doors opened. The man made a strange gesture to ask him to step out. A gesture that was more like a reverence. Hayri felt like he was making fun and insisted on asking him leaving the car first. The door was wide enough to allow them for exiting simultaneously. They began to walk towards the end of the corridor where the cafeteria could be seen behind the windows on the left.

The man started to talk again:

“I grew up without my father. My mother was a diplomat. Me and my little brother, we always traveled with her. We have been in Sofia, Cairo, Johannesburg and Washington. I've always been the dance partner to my mother in embassy balls.”

[8] OECD: Organization for Economic Co-operation and Development

This was the explanation of his ‘reverence’ a moment ago. He continued to speak:

“My father had died in a plane crash, when I was six years old…”

Hayri did not want to hear the rest. He had enough already with his own accident. The eyes of the man they had hit came to his mind. He wanted to change the subject immediately:

“Like most French, do you also like the meat uncooked?” he asked.

He realized his mistake when the noticed the surprised look of the man.

“I mean not overcooked.”

“I'm going to disappoint you, answered the man. Unlike many Frenchmen, I sometimes like it well done. But in France, when you say that in a restaurant, they will think you are an American.”

“But Americans do not necessarily eat the meat well done,” said Hayri.

“It doesn’t matter,” said the man, with a smile. “Here, we believe that all the weird things are done by Americans.”

They were surprised to find the cafeteria full at this hour. Hayri recognized one of the nurses from the floor, sitting at a table talking to a young doctor.

For dinner, they did not have many choices. Hayri ordered a meat dish with fries.

“Would you please cook a little more?” he said to the man who was standing near the fire.

The guy gave him a scornful look. His companion ordered the same dish, not overcooked.

During the meal, they were not too talkative. They exchanged few words.

Leaving the cafeteria Mr. Gouteferd said he would seek a hidden corner for a cigarette. It was a good opportunity for Hayri who wanted to get rid of him. They said "goodnight" and Hayri walked to the elevator.

Arrived at his floor, he exited the elevator and walked to his room. In the hallway he met the same people who were walking slowly, always like a movie in slow motion.

After the distraction of the cafeteria, returning back to the room was boring. He first entered the bathroom to wash his hands. He looked at himself in the mirror, re-examined a few wrinkles and the grey hair.

The night nurse entered in with his medication.

"But you're standing!" she said. "If you want to leave the hospital tomorrow, you should rest."

Was this a blackmail?

"I was in bed for almost two days, madam. I had all the rest I needed."

She handed two pills and a glass of water it.

"This will help you sleep," she said, with an authoritarian tone.

Then she smiled:

"Tomorrow, I'll take you to Mr. Udayasekaran.

"Ah, right?" said Hayri.

"Your doctor must have told you. Before he authorizes your discharge from the hospital, he wants you to meet with Dr. Udayasekaran."

Another blackmail? But he could put on his trousers and jacket and go whenever he wants, right?

Unfortunately it was not that easy, especially with his diplomatic status. A scandal could harm his career.

“Do you know Dr. Udraynaskeran?” he asked.

She corrected:

“Udayasekaran. He is an internationally notorious psychologist. He is of Indian origin.”

“Oh! Really?”

A Turkish guy, having had an accident in France, would therefore see an Indian specialist. What could be the probability of such a coincidence? Was the fate playing a trick on him again?

“So, he is of international reputation” he whispered. “That's all I need.”

The nurse wished him a good sleep and left. Hayri had not yet the desire to sleep. The sleeping pill would have its effect in half an hour or forty five minutes.

He approached the window longing to the see the world. The glass was like a mirror reflecting the light of the room, making the outside completely invisible. He went to the switch and turned off the light. Now he could see the Montparnasse Tower sparkling like a jewel.

He remembered that he had not called his mother. She should be worried by now. He went to the phone and dialed.

Despite the insistence of his mother, he had not yet bought a cell phone. He had no objection to become the '*figlio di mama*[9]' but did not want to ruin his private life with unwanted phone calls.

The phone was picked up at the other end of the line:

"Hayri! How are you, my son?"

She had not even considered necessary to check if it was her son.

"I'm OK mom. I was in the cafeteria. Everything is fine."

"Have you received your laptop?"

"No. With whom did you send it? With Sinan Bey?"

"Yes. He told me he would pass by the hospital tonight to see you again."

Hayri looked at the clock on the wall. It was half past eight.

"No. He did not show up but it doesn't matter. He will probably come to see me tomorrow morning. The nurse gave me a sleeping pill. Tonight, I hope to sleep like a baby."

"Have you talked with the doctor? Are you leaving the hospital tomorrow?"

"I hope so but not sure yet, we'll see. Goodnight mom."

"Goodnight. Sleep well my child, without nightmares."

Hayri was in good mood. He had avoided talking to his mother of his appointment with a psychologist. Everything was already too complicated for her. He did not tell her that tomorrow night he could still be in at the hospital.

[9] figlio di mama (Italian): mama's boy.

He closed his eyes hoping a good sleep.

***

But what kind of sleeping pills did they give him? He could not sleep at all. Well, there was no nightmare, as promised, but he could not get to sleep either!

The phosphorescent quadrant of his watch showed half past nine. The alarm of a car was the only sound that betrayed the silence.

“But this is unacceptable!” he whispered. “That much a noise, close to a hospital? This was incredible.”

He remembered the accident. It was impossible for him to get rid of these images continuing to haunt his brain. Brake squeal, the yell of the driver, the alarm of the other car they struck.

The man they hit was now in a coma. His ghost was in front of his eyes, with the face pressed to the windshield, sliding slowly down.

And this man, now, was somewhere in this hospital! ...

He closed his eyes without being able to empty his brain. Good memories, bad memories; they all came one after the other.

First came his wife. They were walking on a beach in Bodrum[10]. He was holding her hand. Her hand was white as of a Greek statue. This beautiful young lawyer had the cursed power of turning a man, any man, into a slave.

Then it was the divorce. And then this stupid accident that killed her, with her lover at the driver seat.

[10] Bodrum: A favorite vacation town in southern Turkey.

And his daughter, his beautiful little daughter: Seray. So pretty in her ballerina dress. She was dancing, dancing, but all of a sudden, she was becoming invisible. Hayri was searching for her, everywhere.

Suddenly, he felt he could not take any longer! He sat up in bed. This sleeping pill had no effect at all. Perhaps they did not give in sufficient dose. Tomorrow morning, he would talk to the doctor.

He decided to get out of bed and turned the lamp on the nightstand. His bare feet touched the ground. But those pesky slippers, were where they again?

A natural need led him to the bathroom. After his release, he was drawn by the great dark mirror which was replacing the window. He turned off the light and walked to this magical object. His disappointment was great when he approached. Nothing was visible outside. A thick fog had engulfed everything, even the Montparnasse Tower.

He could neither sleep, nor see the outside! An unbearable anguish seized him. What could he do? Would he run out of here, away from the hospital?

...

Suddenly he had an idea, a crazy idea that made him smile.

He searched for his slippers. Opening the door of the room, the bright light blinded him for a moment. He went out into the hallway and walked with small steps first. Then faster and faster. Are the patients allowed to move freely in the corridors, especially at this hour?

"Certainly not!" he muttered, always with a mischievous smile.

Within seconds, he was close to the counter of the night nurse. She was turning her back to the hallway, busy with searching something in the cupboard. A pèlerine[11] was hanging on a hook on the wall. It was one of those coats that caregivers were wearing the nights, especially on cold nights.

So, would he dare? ... Was it a madness? ...

He had no desire to return to the room with the window like a dark mirror. His lips moved silently, and muttered again:

"Why not?"

He took the pèlerine, threw it over his shoulders and walked towards the elevator with quick steps.

No, no, he was not running from the hospital. He had a better idea, a much better idea!

The elevator was waiting on the floor and the doors opened the moment he pressed the call button. Ah, the devil! Was it finally decided to help Hayri? He got in the car and pressed the button marked 'Rez-de-chaussée[12]'.

Upon exiting the elevator, he was surprised by the crowd! Men and women in uniform hastening from all sides. Some had pèlerines like his. Nobody was paying attention to him.

He walked at random. At the intersection of two corridors, he saw a sign, 'ATU[13]'. The noise suggested that the emergency room was there.

A door on his right opened suddenly and he could see the outside. There were ambulances. Blinding lights flashed constantly. Men in white were

[11] Overcoat, used sometimes by doctors and nurses, especially at night.
[12] Ground floor.
[13] ATU: Accueil et Traitement des Urgences (French): Emergency room.

carrying stretchers. The cry of a woman from the emergency room made his hair stand.

The cries of the women always made him lose his composure. He tried to control himself but realized he could not stay here. He retraced his steps to get away.

On his right, a room dimly lit with a green light caught his attention. It should also be an emergency room. Unlike the other, this one seemed calm.

The idea to take a look seemed too bold. But was he not here for some 'fun'?

He looked towards the place he had just left. Several men and women were coming in and out of the emergency room. Cries were heard, stronger this time. He looked back to the room with the green light. It seemed calm and quiet. There was nobody around.

So he entered the room with the green light. A nurse walked out as he entered. She paid no attention to Hayri. Eight beds were lined up against the wall, bathed in the same green light coming from the monitors of the electrocardiographs. They were emitting a continuous 'hmmm...'

He walked along the beds. The first two were held by women. They were all sleeping.

There was a man in the third. He approached. A hose was attached by adhesive plasters out of his mouth. Bandages from his nose and his head were completely hiding his face. This was a thin, dark man.

He continued his 'visit' with the other beds. They were empty or occupied by women. Except the last one, which was occupied by an old man. They all seemed quiet, without much apparent damage.

He returned to the third bed and tried in vain to read folder the hanging at the foot of the bed but the light was poor.

Was this 'the man in coma'? The one they hit by car the other day? ...

He heard footsteps approaching. He put the folder back in its place and headed for the door.

A nurse came as he went out. Once in the hallway, he quickened his pace. He pretended not to hear the voice that shouted "Monsieur?" behind him.

He did not waste time waiting for the elevator. He pushed the door marked 'ESCALIERS[14]' and climbed the stairs as quickly as he could. Once on his floor, he started to run along the hallway. The nurse was not at his post. He hung up the pèlerine in his place, entered his room, closed the door behind him and threw himself into the bed.

A few minutes later he heard footsteps in the hallway and people whispering. The door opened for a couple of seconds then closed.

His heart was pounding. His adrenaline level was at its highest. He remembered the time he was bullying his friends in the dorm, during his high school years.

He smiled. His eyes closed. Now he could sleep.

Damn! The slippers! He had thrown them again under the bed. Couldn't he do things a little orderly?

[14] Stairs

II

Passe passe passera
Le dernier y restera[15]

Skywalk

The slight squeak of the door was enough to wake him. A servant was bringing his breakfast. She put the tray on the sideboard and looked with a smile.

"Hello monsieur. Did you sleep well?"

"Yes, I slept very well, replied Hayri while stretching."

That night, he slept really well. He could also have said "I didn't have a nightmare."

[15] French children song
Pass, pass, all will pass
The last one will stay

He turned his head towards the window. The sunlight hurt his eyes.

The servant pushed the trolley to the bed and helped Hayri to get into sitting position. Then she left the room wishing him a good day.

Hayri growled looking at the large cup of coffee. Hadn't he order tea for breakfast?

"You're not in a hotel room, my friend," he muttered.

He drank half the coffee before he bit the croissant that he found delicious.

"They give this to the patients?" he muttered again.

It was probably his privileged status that earned him this treatment. Moreover, he was not a real patient. After all, he just had a small pain in the neck, right?

He continued drinking the rest of coffee and enjoying the delicious croissant without ceasing to speak. Louder this time:

"It is as if I was at the Café de la Paix."

The people who talk to themselves, aren't they known as 'crazy'? He remember some verses from Orhan Veli[16]:

If I smile when walking alone on the street,
People who see me will think I am crazy.
This idea makes me smile more...

[16] Orhan Veli Kanik (1914 – 1950): A Turkish poet

Finished his breakfast, he got off the bed and looked for his slippers. Another servant entered the room. She was surprised to see him on all fours searching for his slippers.

“Did you lose something, monsieur?” she said with a Portuguese accent.

“I am looking for my slippers, ma'am.”

“They are here, monsieur, under the bed.”

“Ah! I couldn’t see because of my necklace.”

She did not understand the metaphor. He had to explain.

“I just wanted to say that I can’t move my head,” he said, pointing to his neck brace.

“Let me help you,” said the servant.

She leaned across the bed and pushed the slippers with her broom towards him.

“Thank you.”

“You're welcome monsieur.”

And she went into the bathroom to change towels. Hayri put on his slippers and walked to the window. He could see the roofs of the houses and the Montparnasse Tower. He also saw the parking lot for hospital staff. There were two ambulances. Near the wall, which surrounded the parking, there were overflowing trash bins.

Suddenly the alarm of a parked car started to scream. It was difficult to pinpoint the source of the noise. Fortunately, it did not last more than a couple of seconds.

Hearing the door opening, he turned with his whole body to avoid any pain in his neck.

This was the doctor. After a quick exchange of greetings, he said:

“Mr. Alpergun, I have been informed that you slept well last night.”

“Indeed,” replied Hayri.

“No nightmare?”

“None.”

The doctor smiled.

“This is as I expected. We will see if they will return.”

From the beginning, Hayri had noticed that the doctor was avoiding questions about the details of his nightmares.

“Am I leaving the hospital, today?”

The answer came without hesitation.

“In your place, I would stay one more day.”

This was more like an order than a suggestion. But there was nothing to do. The doctor was determined. Hayri had no intention of giving a scratch in his career to avoid a night in this ‘first class hotel’ that he had ‘accidentally’ won.

“Well good,” he said, trying to sound calm. “After all, one night more or one night less. What's the difference?”

The doctor smiled, satisfied.

After a knock on the door, a man entered. He wore on his head a red turban contrasting with his gray suit. He had a red bowtie, which gave him an earlier British colonial elegance. He was obviously from India.

“Mr. Alpergun,” said the doctor. “Let me introduce you Dr. Udayasekaran.”

Hayri shook hands with the newcomer.

“Mr. Udayasekaran is an internationally renowned psychologist,” continued the doctor. “He received his PhD in France and now he continues his experiences with us. We are lucky to have him.”

“Ah!” thought Hayri. “So he has an international reputation and he makes experiences? This is all I needed.”

Mr. Udayasekaran was smiling showing his beautiful white teeth. He said:

“Pleased to meet you, Hayri.”

He had almost no accent, but one would still know eyes closed that he was not French. Hayri did not hide his surprise. This is the first time he was seeing a Hindu speaking French. And he called him “Hayri”, by his first name, like Americans.

“You have an appointment with Dr. Udayasekaran at four o'clock,” said his doctor.

“Four o’clock in my office,” said Dr. Udayasekaran.

“In the other building.” clarified his doctor. “A nurse will accompany you. Your brace will first be replaced with a flexible one. You will be more comfortable.”

Then, two men left. Hayri sat on the bed. Before he takes the time to settle completely, Ahmet, the driver of Madam Consul entered.

"Abi![17] Assalam alaykum[18]. How are you?"

He approached the bed and shook hands with both hands of Hayri, with an exaggerated respect. After the accident, he was probably yelled at by his boss.

"Abi! I brought you some flowers. The concierge did not let me pass with them. He told all visitors: "no flowers in the rooms, please." He told me to leave them on a table near the entrance of the hospital, but I hid the flowers under my jacket," he said.

Proud of his success, he looked for a place to put them.

"You can leave them near the sink in the bathroom. The servant will take care of it," said Hayri.

Ahmet did as he was told and returned.

"Abi, that man, who threw himself in front of us, I heard he's also in this hospital."

"I heard that too," said Hayri.

"Abi, I heard he is in cuma."

"Coma," corrected Hayri.

"What is this, abi?"

"It is a kind of sleep, deep sleep."

---

[17] Abi (Turkish): (Big) Brother. Shows respect (Informal).

[18] An Arabic greeting often used by Muslims around the world. Not necessarily for religious purposes.

"Inshallah[19] he will not die, abi. He threw himself in front of the car, abi. I could do nothing."

Having said that he began to cry. Hayri put his hand on his shoulder and tried to comfort him.

"Allah knows that you are innocent, Ahmet. I told the police that it was not your fault. Thanks for coming to my visit and thanks for the flowers."

Those were the words Ahmet needed to hear, he seemed a little eased.

Hayri felt tired. Fortunately Ahmet had to leave to go to the airport to pick someone coming from Turkey. Before leaving the room, he asked:

"Abi, I just saw a man out of your room. A man with turban, he looked like a fakir. Who was he?"

"A friend of my doctor," said Hayri. He would not give any details. Naturally, he would not say anything to Ahmet about the nightmares, either.

When he was alone, he looked at the wall clock. It was almost 11am. He was beginning to get used to a life without wrist watch. All of his life, he had found watch bands annoying.

This thought reminded him that he also had to get used to not wearing a ring, after the divorce. Another bad memory...

He took a comfortable position in bed. Closed his eyes. Two minutes later, he felt the door open quietly and heard someone enter. This should be the maid. He decided to pretend to sleep. He had no desire to talk with anyone.

The intruder approached to the bed slowly.

---

[19] Hopefully.

"Your eyelids are moving, mon cher. Do you really think you can fool me?"

Hayri opened his eyes. Who could the 'intruder' be other than Sinan Bey?

"Hello Sinan Bey. I was not sleeping. Just resting a bit."

His visitor took out of his bag a pack of Turkish newspapers.

"Sorry I missed our appointment yesterday. I had to go to the Embassy. Then I went home. It was too late to come to your visit. Here, I brought your laptop so that you can stay in touch with civilization."

"Thanks."

"I was expecting to find you on a bed of nails," said Sinan Bey smiling.

"A bed of nails? What do you mean?"

"I met Ahmet in the parking lot. He told me that he saw a 'fakir' coming out of your room."

"Oh, he already knows everything," thought Hayri. He tried to change the subject and opened the package.

"But where is the adapter?"

"What adapter?"

"The adapter of the laptop to connect to the mains."

"Oh? But I thought those things work with batteries."

Was he kidding? One would never know if he was serious or joking. Any case, this was his mother who had forgotten to put the adapter in the package. He still tried to explain:

"The battery is only good for a couple of hours."

Sinan Bey asked with the same wry smile.

“And a fakir, he is ‘good’ for what?”

Hayri decided to explain everything. Sinan Bey listened carefully up to the end, without interrupting.

There was a long silence before Sinan Bey started talking.

“We are old friends, right?” he asked finally.

For Hayri, there was no need to answer this question, their friendship was obvious for both.

“At the university you already knew I was working for MIT[20]. You could at least guess that, right?”

Hayri made an ambiguous sign to say ‘yes’. A sign that could just also be taken for a ‘no’.

“Mon cher, this fakir situations does not please me. I feel there is some kind of abracadabra thing here.”

“Do not be paranoid Sinan Bey. Mr. Udayasekaran is a ...”

The glare of his friend stopped him. He knew he would regret what he had just said but it was too late.

Sinan Bey raised his voice:

“I'm not paranoid, mon cher! And I've never been!”

Yet, this was his nickname in college. One of his nicknames. The other being “cop”, the American word for policeman.

[20] MIT: Turkish Intelligent Service.

Hayri was amused to see him finally losing his temper. Sinan Bey took a few seconds to calm down.

"You are a Turkish diplomat and you represent Turkey. They may try to steal some secret information from you."

"But Sinan Bey, I am not an important person. My title is symbolic. The purpose was only to have a diplomatic passport to avoid the long queues in front of the French Consulate to get their damn visa.

Sinan Bey smiled sincerely.

"*Modesty is the highest form of arrogance*, mon cher."

Hayri had heard this German proverb, perhaps from Sinan Bey himself.

"Well, I'll be discreet when talking to Mr. Udayasekaran. Besides, what can I say? I know nothing. Okay, I worked in Ankara in the Ministry but ..."

"You may actually know more than you think, mon cher. Do you want me to put a bug in your pocket to record your conversation with Mr. Fakir?"

"No, Sinan Bey, please! This is not necessary. I promise to report everything after my visit to Mr. Udayasekaran. OK?"

Sinan Bey made a sign of acquiescence with his head. He remained silent for a few moments with a serious face.

"A commissioner will come to see you."

"I already know that me but nobody came so far."

"He will come this afternoon. I spoke him on the phone."

"Really? Why?"

"He tries to identify the victim of the accident. In about an hour, the Commissioner and I will go to see him together."

"I don't understand. Why would they show you this man? I keep hearing that he is in a coma."

"I already told you. When a car of a diplomat is involved in an accident, they file a case, and since I represent the Embassy of Turkey in this case..."

"Ah! This is a 'case' now?" said Hayri with a wry smile.

Sinan Bey still took his time before speaking. He walked to the window to take a look outside. Then he whirled.

"Mon cher, Hayri. This case may be a bit more complicated than you think."

Did Sinan Bay just resumed his paranoid habits? All that is needed in this case was to close the case as soon as possible. Because diplomats involved in any sort of 'cases' do not have much chance of lasting in the career.

"Sinan Bey, would you please keep me out of all this?"

The response of Sinan Bey was swift.

"But that's exactly what I am trying to do, Hayri!"

***

At three o'clock, guided by a nurse, the Commissioner entered. Hayri was expecting a typical cop popping out of old French movies. He was surprised to see a young man, dressed a little strangely, modern looks, wearing a peak of punk hair. Well, after all, the French Police would not send their best agent for this case that did not matter. Should Hayri take him seriously?

Or, was he wrong? ...

The speech of the Commissioner was actually more serious than his physical appearance. The conversation was brief. Hayri learned from him that they finally have discovered the identity of the injured man. A copy of the report would be submitted to the Turkish Embassy.

Hayri was careful not to ask him any question, in this 'particular' case. He was not even sure if he would have a response. By his diplomatic discipline, he knew he should never say anything more than enough to reporters, to lawyers and especially to the police.

When finished, "I wish you a quick recovery," said the Commissioner, before leaving the room.

Apparently the case was closed without causing other problems. Hayri felt relaxed.

The clock was showing twenty minutes past three. He had forty minutes before his appointment with the psychologist. Eyes closed, he began to exercise to pronounce properly the name of Dr. Udayasekaran. He did not hear the door opening.

"Do you talk in your dreams now, mon cher?

Damn! This was Sinan Bey, again. He thought he was done with him for the day. He opened his eyes slowly.

"Ah! Sinan Bey. I am pleased to see you. Welcome back."

"This one was a 'diplomatic' lie but thank you anyway," replied Sinan Bey, smiling.

"I wasn't sleeping. As you know, I have an appointment with Dr. Udayasekaran at 4pm."

Pleased to have finally got his name pronounced correctly, he sat up in the bed.

“I saw the man you hit”, said Sinan Bey.

Hayri excitedly asked him questions he could not ask the police.

“Is he still in the emergency room? Is he still in a coma?”

“A young woman, his girlfriend, identified him. She is a Lebanese, working in ticket sales for Lebanese Airlines.”

“So he has a girlfriend...” murmured Hayri.

“He is a dark skin, thin man, in his thirties. He has a severe head injury. His head is bandaged, because of fractures.”

“Is he going to survive? What did the doctor say?”

“They do not know yet but they hope he will soon come out of the coma.”

Sinan Bey paused. He was always like that before saying something important.

“He is no longer in the regular emergency room. I heard the Commissioner speaking to a nurse. He was transferred to a single room on the second floor. It seems that last night he had a strange visit.”

The heart of Hayri missed a beat. Sinan Bey continued looking him straight in the eye.

“One of the nurses thought she saw a man standing near his bed.”

Hayri avoided to speak fearing his voice would show his excitement.

"Commissioner called me to say he was waiting for me at the door of the room 234. Two, three, four. Three consecutive numbers."

Was he suspecting Hayri for being the mysterious visitor of last night? And why was he telling him the room number of the man in coma?

"Okay, now I'm going. I'll be back tomorrow to take you home, said Sinan Bey."

"I do not know if Dr. Udayasekaran would want to keep me in the hospital a few more days," said Hayri.

"No, he will not," said Sinan Bey. "I talked to your doctor, you are going to be released tomorrow. Besides, if you were really sick, we would make you first examined by the doctor of the Embassy, and then you would return to Turkey."

Hayri understood right away the gravity of his situation.

"I feel quite normal. I have no more nightmares. Maybe it is no point in seeing this psychologist."

"No, you'll see him," said Sinan Bey, with an authoritative voice. "Then we advise."

The door opened. Hayri looked at the time. It was a quarter to four o'clock. A nurse walked in, pushing a wheelchair.

"Well, now I'm going. Have fun with Mr. Mandrake," said Sinan Bey.

"See you tomorrow," said Hayri."

He was about to get up but the nurse told him to sit.

"I will first change your brace. You'll be better with the new one."

In fact, this one was soft and thinner.

“In a few days, you are not going to wear any brace at all,” said the nurse.

Hayri waited until she finished her job then asked:

“Why is this wheelchair? I can walk without any problem. I even went alone to cafeteria last night.”

The nurse smiled mischievously.

“I know, but tonight you will eat in your room. This is the decision of your doctor and the wheelchair is necessary. We don’t want the patients wandering in hallways.”

Certainly the whole hospital knew! There should be cameras everywhere. Last night, he had been acting like a kid. Apparently, they did not take his act too seriously. For them, Hayri, was just a curious patient and the hospital staff had probably experienced worst cases.

Or maybe he was making up stories. Maybe, they did not know anything, and all these thoughts were only the result of the growing paranoia.

“Please sit.”

The nurse was showing the wheelchair. Hayri got off the bed without the need for assistance and sat down. He tried to hide the smile of a little boy on his face. This would be his first experience with this ‘vehicle’.

“The office of Dr. Udayasekaran is in the other building,” said the nurse, pushing the wheelchair in the hallway.

Hayri remained silent and looked around. Would he be able to find his way back through this maze called ‘Hospital’, if necessary?

"Are you comfortable with your new brace?" asked the nurse.

He answered by turning his head gently:

"Oh, yes ma'am. I feel much better. Thank you."

They approached a frosted glass door. Hayri expected to find an elevator. Normally, to go to the other building, they should descend to the ground floor and go outside. He was even wondering if it was raining.

He was wrong. The sliding door opened automatically and they found themselves in front of a tunnel of glass, illuminated by the daylight.

"We are going pass through the passerelle[21]," the nurse said.

The 'passerelle,' repeated Hayri. He already knew that word. He remembered that he had met it for the first time in a spelling exam, when he was a young student at the French high school in Istanbul. He didn't score well because of this word by writing it as 'passerèle'. And after the exam, he had to look in the dictionary to learn the correct spelling.

Apparently, this one was built between the two buildings, connecting the third floors. It was about two and a half meters in both width and height. And of a length of seven or eight meters. The roof and sides were vitreous.

They advanced in this kind glass tunnel, nurse pushing the wheelchair. On their approach to the end, the doors opened automatically. Once passed, they found themselves in a hallway that seemed very dark compared to luminous skywalk they just left. They advanced about twenty meters and stopped before an elevator.

"We will go up to sixth floor," said the nurse.

[21] French word for skywalk or skybridge.

The door opened instantly. She asked a question while she was entering the cabin:

“You're Turkish, right?”

“Yes, ma'am.”

“I heard you work at the Embassy?”

“No, I work at the OECD. I arrived Paris two months ago, for a three-year mission.

She pressed the button and the car moved off.

“You speak French very well.

“Thank you, Madam. I graduated a French school in Istanbul.”

“Ah! Yes,” she said. “My grandfather told me about that city.”

“Your grandfather?”

“Yes. He was Turkish. He told me all about Istanbul. I would love to see this city one day.”

The elevator stopped. They went out. She continued to tell her story with her grandfather, pushing the wheelchair in the hallway.

“He came to France after World War II and got married with my grandmother who was French. We are Jewish.”

That was explaining her sympathy for Turks.

“Here we are,” she said, stopping in front of a bright red door.

The short ride with the wheelchair was over. Hayri regretted. The nurse told him he could get up. She knocked on the door, opened it without waiting for and answer and told him to enter.

"Dr. Udayasekaran will join you immediately. Make yourself comfortable. I'll come later to take you back to your room."

Then she left, closing the door behind her.

***

First session

Hayri was now alone in the office of Dr. Udayasekaran or Mr. Mandrake, as called by Sinan Bey.

The first thing that sprang to his eyes was the color. Everything was red! The walls, the ceiling, the furniture, the carpets, the curtains. Red everywhere!

"Our man must like this color. I'd like to see what a bull would do here," he thought.

The air was filled with the smell of an oriental perfume. He made a round in the room. It seemed a little large to be a doctor's office and could serve as a meeting room as well.

On his right, a bureau red (obviously), caught his attention. Seven elephants of different sizes were lined up, from the largest to the smallest. They were in walking position, each holding the tail of the other with his trunk.

There was also a gong with radius of about a foot. A wooden hammer was placed on a support.

On his left, he saw a fireplace. He approached to warm hands, instinctively. It was not hot. It was just a decoration!

"Here, you disappoint me Mr. Udayasekaran," he said, aloud.

One of the walls was half covered with a carpet decorated with two beautiful tigers. He approached the large window. He could see the roofs of the houses and behind them the top of the Eiffel Tower. Seen in this way, it was nothing majestic. At this distance, it would look like an electricity pylon.

An inclined chair, reminiscent of a dentist chair, was placed to the right side of the window. On the left, there was a regular chair. Hayri tried to picture Dr. Udayasekaran asking questions to his patients.

He had never talked to a psychologist as a patient before and those he had known by any chance, did not look normal to him.

He walked to the gong and took the hammer with a wild desire to bang, but did not dare. The noise would be heard everywhere. He examined the hammer which seemed made of natural red wood. In fact, he read 'Red Wood' engraved on the handle. He made of movement with the hammer, avoiding to touch the gong. A sound of 'gong!' came out of his mouth. Happy like a child, he returned the hammer to its holder.

A voice coming from behind, scared him:

"You can tap the gong, if you want."

He turned his head suddenly and woke his neck pain. This was Dr. Udayasekaran who was standing at middle of the room.

"You scared me," said Hayri. "I did not hear you entering."

"I did not enter. I was always inside."

"It starts well," thought Hayri. "Here is a man who can become invisible. Is it already an abracadabra trick?"

Dr. Udayasekaran, reading his mind, showed him the rug hung against the wall.

"I was behind the carpet. I was been watching you."

Then he opened the carpet like curtain. There was small alcove large enough to hide a person.

Hayri did not believe what he saw.

"You were watching me? Incredible!"

His heart began to beat wildly. He wanted to make a move toward the door and leave the room but his host was barring the way.

"I beg you," he said. "Will you please stay? I had no bad intentions. It was only part of the first session"

Hayri felt his blood up his head.

"This, this.., this.., is heinous!"

Damn! He was stuttering, again. He has been stuttering in elementary school. His friends were making fun of him. A doctor had told him that learning a foreign language could help. At the age of thirteen, he was able to overcome his disability. But sometimes it was coming back, he never knew when. But especially when he was nervous.

He tried to calm down.

"Sit down, please," said the doctor.

He obeyed and sat on the edge of the tilted chair. He was not at ease. He would leave as soon as the beating of his heart would return to normal.

"Why were you watching me, Mr. Udayasekaran?" he asked, without stuttering to his surprise.

"Call me Nadir please. This is my name. Can I call you by your first name also? It is Hayrettin, right?"

Hayri was calming down. He decided to give himself a few minutes before leaving the room.

"Call me Hayri," he said.

'First name' was an American thing so why did he say that? Was it because his anger was going away, already? Maybe this man had still something magical. Moreover, he was also curious why a psychologist with an international reputation, would watch a patient secretly behind a wall carpet.

Nadir answered this question as if he was reading Hayri's mind:

"People do interesting things when they believe they are not watched. Things that can reveal their character…"

"And what did you learn on my character, Mr. Udayasekaran?"

He did not stutter at all. This helped him recover his self-confidence. He wanted to go on with this game a little longer.

"Nadir. Call me Nadir please."

Hayri nodded in agreement with his head.

“You have the character of a child. You'll never grow old,” said the doctor, with a smile.

While Hayri was wondering if he should take these words as a compliment or an insult, Nadir handed the gong hammer.

“Take this and, hit the gong!”

Hayri could not help laughing.

“Oh, no. I don’t want to do that.”

Nadir continued to hand him the hammer.

“Of course you do! Take it!”

But this man was serious. Was he a little crazy like everyone involved in psychology?

“Maybe next time,” he said, a little sharply.

Did he just say ‘next time’?

“What you want to do with me, monsieur Udayasekaran?” asked Hayri.

‘Nadir, please,’ he insisted with a grin.

Then he pointed to the chair.

“Can we exchange seats please?”

The ‘patient’ obeyed and sat down on the chair by the window, while the psychologist settled on the ‘dentist’ chair.

“We exchange roles?”

“Only for today,” said Nadir.

"But why?"

"With my visitors - I do not like to use the word 'patient'- I must establish a complete confidence. If not, my method does not give results. So, we exchange roles in this first session and I tell my visitors everything they want to know about my life. You can't trust a person if you do not know him enough. Don't you think so?"

Hayri thought he would probably regret not having left the room earlier. It was a little late now. He decided to participate in this comedy for a couple of more minutes, curious to see the limits of his own patience.

"What do you expect me to do? Am I supposed to ask you questions?"

"There is no rule, Hayri. I am going to tell you my story. You can stop me and ask questions whenever you want."

He closed his eyes and began to speak in a soft voice of a speaker talking on the radio.

"I was born in Ceylon. This is an island about 30 kilometers of south-east of India. This is a country we call Sri Lanka."

"What is it?" wondered Hayri. A lecture of geography?

"My father was also born in Ceylon. At the age of nineteen, while on a trip to Bangkok, he met my mother, who was Vietnamese."

This was explaining why he knew French.

"After I was born, my parents lived thirteen years in Sri Lanka."

Having said that, Nadir remained silent.

Hayri asked:

"What happened after? Have they left the island?"

Nadir opened his eyes and looked Hayri, as if he is surprised of his presence. Had he forgotten that he was not alone in the room?

"One evening, a man entered the house by breaking the door and murdered my father, in front of my eyes…"

***

The session had lasted much longer than he had expected. Hayri was curious to know what the time was but he had left his watch in his room. He could ask Nadir but it was too late. He was already out of his office. He wouldn't knock the door back to ask him the time.

"What's the point of knowing the time?" he thought. After all, he was in a hospital and the hours were flowing slower than the outside world, weren't they?

So, Dr. Udayasekaran and Hayri had both same fate. Both fathers were murdered. Hayri confessed himself that he had found much more than he was expecting with this first session. He had even promised to return tomorrow afternoon for another session, after his discharge from the hospital.

The wheelchair that took him so far was folded and waiting against the wall, but the nurse was not in sight. She should be waiting somewhere nearby and would come back any minute.

Another trip to his room in the chair did not seem amusing at all. He could walk back. But he had to flee quickly, before the nurse came.

He walked to the elevator on the run. The cabin was on the floor and the doors opened as soon as he pressed the call button. It was his lucky day. Once inside, he pressed the button for the third floor.

He said, «quick, quick!» for closing the doors as soon as possible, before the nurse would take him in the act of escape. Doors played the game, the cabin moved. A few seconds later, doors opened back at the third floor.

He left quickly and headed for the skywalk. He was embarrassed for what he did but he never imagined that running away from a nurse would be that exciting.

The automatic doors opened on his approach. "It's like an amusement park," he thought.

Crossed the threshold, he stopped. There was something odd. He peered forward, then back, but saw no difference. His doubt was strengthened more when he walked two steps in this sort of tunnel. There was something wrong with this skywalk. Maybe with the nurse, they had used another one. He pressed his nose to the window, looked right and then left to see if there were another skywalk but there wasn't any in sight.

This one was not as illuminated as the 'other' one. However, since his last visit, the sky had cleared. He could even see the sunlight piercing the clouds in some spots.

Suddenly he thought he heard voices and footsteps ... They were coming from the ceiling. The ceiling was not made of glass like the other one!

It took him a few seconds before he realized that the skywalk had two decks! He was in the bottom deck. Earlier, with the nurse, they had used the upper deck.

How come that he had not noticed it before? “He”, who thought was an intelligent man and a good observer? He couldn’t help to make fun of himself.

Though, there was one last point to be clarified. He was sure he pressed the third button in the elevator.

He walked back in the old building to read the number of the floor. He saw «3rd floor» clearly marked. There was no error.

He returned to the skywalk. When he looked to the ground, he saw clearly the difference in levels between the new and the old building which caused a shift between the floors. The second and third stages of the new building, were respectively connected to the third and fourth floors of the old building.

As there was nothing to do, he continued his way towards the new building. He should be in second floor. He walked down the hallway in front of him in the hope of finding an elevator to the third floor, where his room was.

He felt tired. An elevator, you can’t find it when you need. Maybe at the end of the hallway?

Rooms were aligned on the left and the right. He could read the numbers of doors: 245, 244, 243 ... It was well in the second floor.

He could read from a distance, towards the end of the hallway, a bright sign: ASCENSEURS[22].

[22] Elevators

"Finally," he thought.

When passing in front of one of the rooms, he saw a policeman, sitting in a chair placed next to the door. Who could be the person staying in this room? A convict?

He read the number on the door with surprise: 234. This was the room Sinan Bey had mentioned. The room numbered with consecutive digits: 2, 3 and 4. The room he was standing in front, was the room of the man in coma! The man his driver had almost killed!

Damn! Being caught here could get him in trouble. He quickened his walk.

He was surprised when he found himself in front of a large window with a view towards the Montparnasse Tower. This was the end of the hallway. He had missed the elevator.

Wasting no time, he walked in the opposite direction, head down. Was he being watched? Were there hidden cameras everywhere?

Just steps to the elevator, he looked forward. «Curiosity killed the cat, right?» he said, to himself. He was now about fifteen yards away from the policeman who was sitting in front the room 234.

When pressing the button of the elevator, he saw a woman leaving the room. She said something to the policeman. Hayri could hear the word «water». The policeman showed her the fountain near the elevator. She began to walk towards Hayri.

She was very close when the doors opened. While Hayri was entering, they both looked for a moment in each other's eyes. She was a young brunette. Beautiful, one could say. The doors closed and the cabin moved.

He had seen her already, somewhere… But where?

The elevator stopped. A group of nurses entered the cabin. Hayri realized that this was not his floor. He had not even pressed the button for the third. He was at the fifth floor. The doors closed immediately leaving him out. He had to wait for the next.

Alone in front of the elevator, he thought of this woman. She had green eyes. A brunette with green eyes! He wouldn't see one every day, would he? So, where did he see her?

The elevator did not take long to come back. He entered. The devil told him to press the button of the second to go and see that woman again, but he pressed the third. Didn't he have enough excitement already, for today?

III

Sleeping is a waste of time
I am afraid of sleeping
It is a form of death.

Edith Piaf

The Man in Coma

The Portuguese lady who brought him breakfast put the tray on the small table. The service table with wheels was removed. It was no longer needed.

As the patient did not look good, she avoided conversation and walked out without delay.

Hayri approached and looked at his breakfast.

"Coffee? Again?" he said, disappointed.

He put some butter on the bread and bit. Then he walked to the window. This morning, the view was limited due to rain. He could barely perceive the cars in the parking lot.

The phone rang. This would be his mother. He walked to it without hurry and answered.

"Hello?"

"Hello my son. How are you? Are you all right?"

"Hi mom. I am okay. Don't worry."

"Did you sleep well?"

Being forced to start his day with a lie was not fun. Last night he did not take the pill that the nurse had given him. He had taken it into his mouth, but spat it as soon as she had left the room.

He was feeling so good before going to bed that he took the risk, believing that the nightmare would not come back.

But the 'thing' had returned. He woke up several times with horrible screams but nobody came to check on him.

"What will I do?" he murmured desperately.

"What did you say, Hayri? I did not hear."

Damn! He had forgotten that his mother was at the other end of the line.

"Nothing mom, I talk to myself. This is because of the breakfast. When I come home, I want you prepare some tea for me. And I want to eat bread with Turkish white cheese. I do not want any meal, neither from Turkish cuisine nor French. Just regular Turkish breakfast, please!"

“Don’t worry Hayri. I can find everything you like at the Greek grocery store around the corner. I already bought a packet of the cheese you like. And I will make the tea too. At what time are you going to be discharged from the hospital?”

“I am waiting for the doctor. But I won’t be home before 5pm, or maybe 6pm. Because I'm going to see another doctor.”

“Why?”

Oops! This was a mistake to tell her that. She would worry now and it would be very difficult to calm her. He had make up something, and fast.”

“This is a friend of my doctor. He wants to visit Turkey this summer. I'll give him some advice.”

He congratulated himself for this excellent lie.

“Oh, really? But why?”

Like all mothers, she was too curious about everything concerning her son.

“Mom, why don’t we talk about it when I am back home? I need to shave before the doctor arrives. See you later. Goodbye.”

He hung up to avoid more questions.

He went into the bathroom and looked in the mirror. His chin looked like the back of a porcupine. But the shaver did its job and within minutes and the chin turned into a polished apple.

When he returned to the bed the phone rang again. Worried that this could still be his mother, he hesitated a little. When he finally picked up, the voice of Sinan Bey reassured him.

“How are you?” asked his friend.

Without waiting for a reply, he continued:

“I talked to your doctor. You are going to be discharged today.”

“Is that so?”

Wasn’t he supposed to be the first one to know that? The doctor could at least have the courtesy of telling him too.

“So you have another appointment with the fakir from India at 3pm?”

That was a little too strong.

“You are better informed than me Sinan Bey. Could also tell me please what am I going to have for dinner?”

Sinan Bey ignored the sarcasm.

“This is not all,” he said. “I would not be surprised if the same commissioner comes back to see you.”

“Really? Why?” said Hayri, surprised.

“It is only a possibility. But stay in zota[23]”.

He was speaking in slang using it as a coded language. They used to do that when they were students at the university. Apparently he was not pleased with the visit of the Commissioner. Hayri wandered what would he say if he had seen the punk guy?

“Do you think you would be done with your fakir, at 4pm? I'll pick you up to take home.”

[23] Zota (Slang, Turkish): stay discrete/safe.

“Thanks Sinan Bey. That's nice. I'll be in the other building. It has separate parking lot.”

“Don’t worry, I'll find out,” he said, and hung up.

After the phone conversation Hayri wanted to return to the window. But he changed his mind when the alarm of the same car (he thought it was the same) started to scream.

“It's unbelievable, in the parking lot of a hospital! How can there be such irresponsible people,” he said.

“You're right, replied a voice.”

It was his doctor.

“Hello Mr. Alpergun. I'm sorry for that noise. The management of our hospital will take care of this as soon as possible.”

Hayri did not answer. He even skipped to return his greeting. The doctor noticed the nasty look of Hayri.

“I am also sorry for not having come sooner to tell you that you are going to be discharged today.”

Hayri replied rather curtly.

“I know A little bird has already told me.”

The doctor pretended not to notice his attitude.

“I hope you had a good sleep last night?”

"Was this a trick question?" wondered Hayri. Despite an education in political science, he had never been a good liar. Never a good poker player either.

He decided to try demagoguery:

"Thanks to Dr. Udayasekaran."

His cheeks betrayed him by turning pink. The doctor was kind enough not make him feel that he had noticed the change in color.

"I talked to Mr. Udayasekaran. He also seemed pleased with your session."

Hayri tried this time a forced smile.

"He told me about his life: his childhood, his education."

"I know. He has 'his' methods."

Dr. Udayasekaran had even told Hayri about his first love, but it was not necessary to repeat all this.

"Today, we are going to have second and final session," said Hayri.

The doctor looked surprised.

"I doubt it. Dr. Udayasekaran told me that you would need at least ten sessions. You are 'physically' in the form, at least you will be. Then, we will remove your neck brace, but..."

Doctor had stresses the word 'physically'. Hayri felt blushed to the ears. He felt like a student who had passed his physics school test but failed in psychology class.

He reacted:

"Ten more sessions?"

Were they trying to squeeze a little more money from the insurance?

His nightmare of last night came to his mind. His condition was not normal at all. And if the situation was worsened? ...

The doctor handed him a paper.

"This is a copy of your prescription medications. Before leaving, stop by the pharmacy."

"Can I go now?"

"If I were you, I would not hurry. Your discharge order will not be ready for another two hours. As you have your appointment with Dr. Udayasekaran this afternoon, you can relax in the room. Any case, it is paid for today."

Was he joking? This was not a hotel room.

"Well, in the meantime, can I have lunch in the cafeteria?"

"That's a good idea. I think they have the Breton cake for dessert today."

The phone rang. The doctor shook his hand.

Come to see me this Monday. We will take your brace off," he said before leaving.

The person at the phone was Sinan Bey again.

"About two o'clock, someone from Embassy will be present at the reception of the hospital. This will probably be Mehlika Hanim. She will help you with your exit formalities, insurance etc."

Having said that, he hung up.

The name reminded his aunt. Her name was Mehlika too.

'Mehlika Sultan!' This is how he used always called her. She was only eight years older then Hayri. For him, she was more of a big sister than an aunt.

"I have to call her one of these days," he murmured.

He had known another person who had the same name. But who? He could not remember.

A slight gurgling from his stomach reminded him that he was hungry. On the wall, the clock showed almost noon. He began to dress. He felt in a good mood. He put his pants that seemed less comfortable than his 'hospital uniform' but now, he was free.

There has been a knock at the door. Who could that be? Nurses did never take the trouble to knock before entering.

Two men entered. Hayri recognized the punk-commissioner of yesterday. The other, who looked older, had more serious look. He wore a gray suit and a red tie.

"This chamber receives as many visits as the reception desk of a hotel," thought Hayri.

After exchanging greetings, the punk-commissioner introduced his colleague. He was a Commissioner of Police like him. His name was Mr. Huot.

"I'm in charge of this case Mr. Alpergun," said the newcomer.

"Ah! They send two commissioners now? They have nothing more serious to do at the Police?" thought Hayri.

He remembered the advice of his friend Sinan Bey. He would be discreet.

"I've already made my statement," he said, unable to stop looking at the red tie of the second man.

"I know," said the man, in a respectful manner.

Then he pulled something out of his wallet. This was a photo. He showed it to Hayri.

"Do you know this man, monsieur?"

Hayri leaned over to look. It was the passport size photo of a man he did not know.

"No," he said.

"This is the photo of the man who almost died in the accident. He is still in coma," said the Commissioner with the red tie.

With that, Hayri fetched his glasses and looked closely. This was the picture of a thin, dark haired man of about thirty years.

"No, I've never seen him," he said.

The two commissioners exchanged a quick glance. Hayri noticed their reaction.

"Is there a reason for me to know him? Do you have any information that I don't know?" he asked.

This direct question almost startled the man with the red tie.

"No, monsieur. This is a standard questions we ask everyone after accidents."

And he smiled for the first time since he had entered the room.

“I think I already clearly said in my statement that I was in the back seat of the car when accident happened. I was reading a newspaper and I didn’t see anything,” said Hayri in a dry voice.

This was lie. He had seen the eyes of the man, his face pressed to the windshield. Of course one should never say such things to the police, especially when they seek a calf under the ox[24].

On this, the commissioners wished him a good recovery and left. They were more polite when leaving then their arrival.

Hayri decided to leave the room as quickly as possible. He no longer had any desire to eat. “The Breton cake, it will be for another time,” he said aloud. He dressed quickly and shoved the rest of his things into his backpack. He would spend rest of his time in the waiting room.

The door opened and a nurse came to her surprise, with a wheelchair. Then she said with an exaggerated smile:

“So, you leave us today?”

“Yes, ma'am, I'm leaving now. But what is this?” he asked, pointing to the chair. “This is not for me, I hope?”

“It is for you, monsieur. The discharged patients are rolled up like that on their way out. This is the house rule. Besides, I will also help you to complete your paper work,” she said.

There was nothing to do, the lady seemed quite determined. He obeyed without resistance.

[24] Looking for something in the wrong place. (Turkish expression)

***

Hayri thanked Miss Mehlika for coming from the Embassy to help for formalities. Her French was impressive. She looked like a real Parisian woman.

Upon leaving the hospital, they shook hands and she walked to her car. Hayri watched her for a few moments from behind, trying to guess her age.

He was happy to leave the hospital. It was cold outside. Fifty yards was separating him from the entrance of the old building. His mother had asked him to send his raincoat but he had refused; just by need to tell her “no!”. He did not want to be controlled by women. He always liked to do the opposite of what they told him. And this was one of the reasons that his wife left him, wasn’t it?

No. He knew that this was not the real reason. There were many other things that he did not want to remember. It wasn’t the time to analyze the past. He raised the collar of his jacket, put his hands in his pockets and began to walk along the wall.

Arrived at the alley between the two buildings, cold air slapped his face.

Here! There was a red light in front, a human shaped figure was asking him to wait. But this was narrow way than only one car could pass at a time. There was no car in sight. Would he ignore that stupid signal and cross the street, of only two meters wide?

Being a ‘civilized’ man, he decided to wait and began a dance of American Indians hopping on his feet. But it did not help much. The red man on the pole did not turn green.

“I give you ten more seconds, red man,” he said.

He raised his head as much as his brace allowed him and watched the skywalk up on his left and whispered: “I should have to go through it.”

That way he would not have cold and he would not have to wait before the red light.

From there, you could see that the skywalk had well two decks. It was connecting the second and the third floors of the new building, respectively to the third and fourth of the old. And he clearly observed the difference between the levels, which was the reason for this discrepancy.

He noticed a button on the pole beside him and read: “Press the button to cross.”

The man turned from red to green when he pressed.

“What a fool I am,” he said.

He received a drop of rain on the nose. He began to run. The rain almost caught him when he pushed the revolving door of the entrance.

He found himself in a hall that reminded him of nothing a hospital.

“Monsieur, you are here for?” asked the young girl on reception.

“I have an appointment with Dr. Udayasekaran. I'm Alpergun.”

After consulting a notebook, she said:

“I see no appointments for Dr. Udayasekaran.”

“It starts well,” thought Hayri. Should he go through the skywalk to avoid this silly girl?

“Please look again, he said,” without bothering to hide his irritation.

“One moment please,” she said.

After a few phone calls everything was settled. She showed him the elevators:

“Sixth floor.”

Two minutes later, Hayri was in front Nadir’s door. He hesitated before knocking. The easiest thing to do would be to turn his back and walk away.

“But why?” he thought, smiling. The doctor would not chew him up.

And then he remembered what his gym teacher in high school had told: “Turks are the bravest nation in the world!”

Then he ‘bravely’ knocked the door.

Nadir’s voice was heard:

“Come in!”

***

Second session

The scent in the air was not the same, but it was pleasant.

“Hello Hayri, how are you?” asked Nadir.

“I am all right,” doctor.

“Today is your turn. Are you ready to tell me the story of your life?”

Hayri would have liked to say ‘no’ but the last time he was here, he had promised to tell him everything. So, he made a sign of affirmation with his head he regretted immediately. He had a sore neck.

For some reason, this man inspired him more confidence than any other person he knew before.

He lay down on the inclined chair and began to talk.

“I was born in Ankara, the capital of Turkey.”

“Is this the city that we know under the name Angora?” asked Nadir.

“Yes, but I think Angora is rather European pronunciation. Local people pronounce it as ‘Angara’.”

“But Ankara was not always the capital of Turkey, right? I think Istanbul was the …”

Hayri interrupted him.

“Ankara is the capital of Turkey since the first day of the republic. Istanbul was the capital of the Ottoman Empire, but not of the modern Turkey.”

That's it, he was beginning again. Whenever someone asked a question on Turkey, he was starting to talk. He could even begin to tell the whole story of the Ottoman Empire.

But he had to go to the ‘serious stuff’. It was not the Turkey that was lying on the inclined chair. It was him.

“I can say that I had a happy childhood. At that time, in Ankara, there was a lot of empty spaces between the buildings. We children were playing all kinds of games, especially foot.

He tried to turn his head to look at Nadir.

"By foot[25], I meant soccer."

"I know," said Nadir, with an encouraging smile.

The Doctor was a really nice man. Hayri was feeling that he could tell him all his life.

"One day, when I was the goal keeper, I got shot on my face by the ball and it was the end of my soccer career. I was seven."

Nadir had a short laugh. Then he asked:

"Did you always live in Ankara, during your childhood?"

Hayri continued:

"My father was assigned as deputy governor to Diyarbakir. He was initially reluctant to take my mother and me with him. After a democratic vote, two against one, the family decided to stay together. We went to the East of Turkey, for one year. This was an unforgettable time in my life."

"Why?"

"In this city everything was different. In the streets, there were men wearing turbans. (Damn! He should say that Nadir has one too). They were guiding their camels. When they spoke, they had an accent. To understand them, I should pay attention. We stayed in a hotel for a couple of weeks before moving into an apartment. It was late summer. It was very warm. The first thing that struck me were the cockroaches. They were twice the size of those I knew. I found disgusting. I was always afraid of insects. And I was

[25] Foot: abbreviation for football (soccer) in French.

traumatized when I was told that this city was famous for its scorpions. I even remember begging my parents to return to Ankara because of this."

Nadir could not help smiling. Hayri smiled too.

"Did you go to school there?"

"Yes, I was in elementary school. I was a good student, I loved my teacher and my friends. I was happy."

"Tell me about your friends."

"The boys were all bigger and stronger than me. There was even one that had the mustache."

"A student with mustache? In elementary school?"

"Shocking isn't it? My mother would not let me out to play with the neighborhood boys. Sometimes my school friends came to get me off the house. So she left me reluctantly. I did not understand some of these boys when they talked to me. One of them explained me that they were speaking Kurdish. Over time, I even learned a few words: I could say "vara, vara" which means "come, come" in Kurdish.

They both smiled again.

"I especially loved their hair style. It was cut short in the neck and temples, but left long above the head, as if they had a straw hat. When they made a sudden move to turn the head, the long hair was opening like the skirt of a rotating dancer. I envied them. I wanted my hair to be cut like them but my mother refused."

"You must have several memories of those days. Will you tell me one?"

"Okay. Once upon a time…."

He looked to see if Nadir smiled. Instead, he seemed serious. This was not the time for jokes.

"As I said earlier, there were a few in the class that were older students. Three of them were real adults, they looked like men. Their studies were probably interrupted several times. This is why they were still in primary school. Since the primary education is compulsory in Turkey, they kept coming; until the age of sixteen."

"At what age do you start school?"

"Normally, at seven. But in eastern Turkey, things are a little different. Newborns sometimes take the identity of their big dead brothers. A five year old child can have the birth certificate of one of the ten years."

"But why?" asked Nadir.

"Because people are lazy to go to the town for just a certificate, they prefer to stay in their village and use the certificate of the big brother who died."

"And the government does nothing about that?"

"The authority of the government can't reach some remote corners of the country."

He stopped talking for a moment. Did he really say that? As a state official, especially as a diplomat in mission in a foreign country, he should be cautious with his words when criticizing his own country?

His eyes met those of Nadir. He was listening carefully.

“Three of the oldest students were sitting at the back of the class. Each one on a different bench. As it was impossible to know their true ages, because of the ‘borrowed’ certificates of deceased brothers. The school was tolerating their existence. And it was perhaps better that they come to school, rather than wandering the streets.

Hayri looked Nadir. Apparently he was sharing his opinion.

“These three boys were called Feridun, Rashad and Ibrahim. They were staying away from others. Feridun was never smiling. He was the one who had the mustache.”

“One day in class of Turkish grammar, we were reading a story. There was the word ‘sulky’ in a sentence. The teacher asked us to make another sentence with this word. I immediately raised my hand and said, ‘*Feridun is a sulky boy!*’

“There was a burst of laughter in the classroom. I looked Feridun to see his reaction. He looked mad.

“On leaving the school, I had totally forgotten this event. I was walking towards home, when he cut me off. I immediately saw the danger. I turned around and started running towards the school, hoping to find refuge there. But this time I saw Rashad and Ibrahim walking towards me. I was panicked. I took the first side street at random and I continued to run. I was looking back regularly. Feridun and others were following me.

“I was running like a gazelle in the narrow streets of the old town. Feridun and others following me like lions. And they were closing the distance!

“I was suddenly forced to jump over a large dislocated fence that was barring my way. Feridun, who was just right behind me did not notice it and fell down. I was breathless. I stopped. I was praying god he doesn’t beat me.

“But the others, instead of following me, pounced on Feridun. This is at this moment that I realized they were trying to save me.

“I was tired to the point that my feet did not move. Feridun, immobilized by the other two, showed me his fists and was throwing insults. This was the first time I was seeing someone hating me. I was terrified. I was never been so scared. This has been the day I learned that you can have enemies as well as friends.

“I finally arrived home. I lied to my mother about what happened. I told her that I had played soccer.

“The next day, the three boys did not come to school. Witnesses to the incident had informed my father. He had talked to the governor and an administrative circular was distributed to all schools to comply with the age limit provided by law. The big boys would no longer come to school. Their education was over. I felt sorry for them. I felt a little guilty. That day, I was saved by Rashad and Ibrahim. If I had not said this word for Feridun, none of this would have happened.

“Did you see them again?” Nadir asked.

“I saw Rashad, the day of our departure from Diyarbakir. And a few years later in high school, and then in the same university. He had found a way to continue his studies. Well, it's a long story.”

There were a few seconds of silence, then Nadir spoke:

"The nightmares that you have after your accident, do you think they are connected to this event?"

"I do not think so," replied Hayri with a surprised look.

Nadir smiled.

"Then, there is something else. We will find out." he said.

***

Before leaving the building, he looked through the glass of the revolving door. Apparently the rain had given way to the cold wind. When he looked at the clock on the wall he was surprised. It was almost 5pm. He had spent two hours with Nadir.

The headlights of a car in the parking lot flickered. This was be Sinan Bey. He saw him and waving. Once outside, he ran zigzagging between parked cars. The left car door opened at his approach. He entered immediately.

"Brrr! Winter has already arrived," he said, rubbing his arms.

"Not yet. This is only the beginning of October. We will have good days before winter comes," said Sinan Bey.

He started the car.

"So? Your interview with the fakir, how was it?"

"Interview? But Sinan Bey, it was not an interview. It was a psychological therapy session or rather 'psychotherapy'."

“Come on, mon cher. ‘The psych…’, a word can’t even pronounce correctly, is not a science. It is only an illusion show. This is nothing but a ‘mumbo jumbo’ and it should never be taken seriously.

“Before I knew Nadir, I was thinking the same way.” Said Hayri

“What is ‘Nadir’? His first name? Do you talk each other by first names, like Americans? So he calls you, Hayri?”

Hayri was accustomed to his friend's way of talking. One had to be patient with him.

“It doesn’t matter, Sinan Bey. He is a well-educated man. He is not a magician and he does not pull rabbits from a hat. I have respect for him. Anyway, this was the first and the last session.

“Oh, really? I began to doubt if this fakir hypnotized you?”

Hayri laughed.

“Excuse me, but you just tell me that you do not consider psychology as a science, and now you talk about hypnosis. So what makes you think that ‘hypnosis’ exists? According to you, is it not another mumbo jumbo too?”

Sinan Bey pulled the car backwards from the parking spot nervously, then began to roll slowly towards the exit.

“If you have problems that you want to forget, mon cher, I know of only one way. You buy a French baguette, a bottle of red wine and some cheese. You put them on the table and you start to enjoy. You'll see, your problems will vaporize.”

“But this is a classic French method,” said Hayri laughing.

He had the idea to invite him home.

"I am sure my mother prepared a nice dinner for my home return, with raki[26] and white cheese. She would be happy if you join us. How about you join me for a Turkish method?"

"Thanks for the invitation but I have to go to the Embassy for a meeting. It will be for another time."

"A meeting? At this hour?"

"There is never a precise time for meetings concerning security."

They were out of the parking lot and they were riding down the street. Suddenly a motorcycle passed their car and raked in front of them. Sinan Bey yelled:

"Punk!"

The heart of Hayri began to beat hard.

"Could you please drive slowly, Sinan Bey?"

"I wasn't speeding!"

"I know but I still have the effects of the accident on me. Anything can scare me."

Hayri had slightly stuttered when he was speaking. "I hope it is not coming back," he said to himself. Sinan Bey gave him a quick nervous look. They have been silent for a few minutes.

It was Friday. It was five thirty pm and traffic jams in the streets of Paris were exceptional.

---

[26] Turkish popular alcoholic drink

"I understand. Maybe it would be better you continue to consult this psychologist," said Sinan Bey seriously.

"No, no. This was the last session. I'm not going to see him again. It's over."

"Unless the nightmares come back," he thought. Sinan Bey even gave him a strange look.

"What did you do during the sessions?"

Hayri had no desire to talk about the session.

"I'll tell you later," he said.

"Okay."

Again there was silence. It lasted a little longer this time. Then Sinan Bey started to talk:

"The police told us that the passport of the man you hit, is false."

"Really?" asked Hayri, surprised.

"At the Embassy I saw a fax sent by the French Police. They distribute the photograph of the man to all embassies of Middle Eastern countries, to find out his true identity. His girlfriend was cooperating but it seems she does not know too much either. If one relies on the information of his passport, the guy came to France only a couple of months ago."

Hayri wanted to tell Sinan Bey that he had seen a woman, probably the girlfriend, last night near the room of the man in a coma. Her green eyes were engraved in his memory. And he had probably seen her before, somewhere but he could not remember where.

However it would not be wise to say such a thing to Sinan without triggering one of his fits of paranoia. He would make a fuss.

Sinan Bey had more to say.

“Police found a new witness to your accident. Rather two witnesses. An American couple.

“Oh, really? But where were they up to until now?”

“It seems that they are tourists visiting Paris. They took pictures of the bridge just before the accident.”

“Really? Did they take the picture of the accident?

“No. Well, I do not think so. But they saw the accident. And after the accident they returned to their hotel.”

“Why didn’t they talk to the police on the spot?”

“Just after the accident, there were people around car. The American couple may have thought there could be many other people who had seen the accident. As a matter of fact, there was at least ten witnesses. But none of them had seen what the Americans pretended to have seen.”

“Sinan Bey! Would you please tell me what they saw?”

He did not answer immediately. Hayri was impatient. Fortunately, his friend was not long to respond.

“The Americans have said that the man had deliberately thrown himself in front of your car, as if he wanted to commit suicide.”

Hayri was chocked.

"Ahmet the driver told me the same thing, when he was visiting me at the hospital. I thought he was making it up to save his skin. But how do you know all this? It is the police who told you that?"

"You bet! No police will tell you things that witnesses reported. I learned from ..."

At this time his cell phone rang. He waved his hand to let Hayri know he would finish later, then answered the call.

"Selamun aleykum[27]. What is it?"

He listened without saying a word. Then hung up.

They drove in silence for a few moments, then Sinan Bey found a parking spot and stopped.

"What's happening Sinan Bey. Why are we stopping?"

"Have you ever heard of the 'Nail'?"

"The Nail?"

"This is the name of our secret service in France."

"So, we have a 'secret service' in France. Why do they call the Nail?"

"All countries of the world have secret services, mon cher. You do know how to play poker, right?"

"You know that I was playing, when I was in college."

"The cheater in poker make marks on cards with their nails. Minor marks that you can't see if you do not pay close attention. That's how they

[27] salute

recognize the cards. The Nail is formed like that, all alone. This is not a service organized by the MIT[28]. These are the Turkish residents who began to exchange information. Finally, they began to pass us information they were gathering."

"But what about the French Contre-Espionage? They do nothing?"

"Here mon cher, we are talking about 'open information', available to everyone. You could probably read all of it in the newspapers, the next day. Even the French secret service benefits from this."

Hayri turned his head to the other side to hide his grin. This 'secret service' looked more like a club of old gossipy women.

Then he asked chuckling:

"And what news have you just received from the 'Nail', Sinan Bey?"

"They called me in order to give a very interesting information. Besides the Americans, the police questioned another witness: a drunk man who lives on the banks of the Seine River, near the bridge. French call such men 'clochards'. And according to this clochard, someone threw an object into the river just before the accident."

"So what?

"The police think he's our guy. The guy who is in a coma now."

"Really? And what did he threw?" Hayri asked curiously.

Sinan Bey took a few seconds as usual, before answering.

[28] MIT (Milli Istihbarat Teskilati): Turkish Intelligent Service.

“That's what the divers of the Police are searching now. We do not know yet.”

Forever I shall be stranger to myself
Albert Camus

IV

Boomerang effect

“Thank you Madam Consul, thank you very much,” said Hayri, hanging up the phone.

This was nice of her to call him to wish a good recovery. She told him that the meeting of the International Committee was postponed. Hayri had no reason to worry. She would send him the folder. He would have enough time to prepare his report when he would back at work. But now, he should rest a few days. This what she had advised.

Her name was Melahat, the Turkish Consul in OECD. She was the one who had invited him to Paris for this mission. She had been a student of his father, at the years when he was teaching at university.

Ever since Hayri was home, he remained lying on the couch, watching TV with the remote control in hand. He was eating without objecting everything his mother was bringing. He had received a few calls from friends.

“I'm getting fat,” he told his mother.

“It makes you good. You're too skinny.”

According to his mother, he had always been too skinny. And now, thanks to his mom, he could turn into a sumo wrestler.

He was glad to be back home. His mom had prepared an excellent dinner.

He would like to have a glass of wine, but when he was about to get a bottle, he remembered that he had to take a sleeping pill before bed. Taking both together could be dangerous. The small battle between the sedative and in his consciousness ended up with the sad victory of the sleeping pill. That night, he wanted to sleep, without any nightmare!

Connecting to Internet in order to check his emails did not seem interesting at all. He just put on his pajamas and sat down in front of the TV. He loved to do that from time to time. His wife was going crazy when she saw him like that in his pajamas in the living room of the house. But that was long ago, before the divorce, before she died.

He tried to focus on the news on TV. Minister of Internal Affairs was spoking about the riots in the suburbs of Paris. The few days he spent in hospital had been enough to keep him away from the real world. He was not aware of what was happening.

He began to play with the remote control. On one channel, there was a documentary program about rugs. He waited in vain for fifteen minutes in the hope to see some Turkish carpets, then continued his zapping.

His mother's voice startled him:

“Do not sleep on the couch! Go to your bed room!”

This was like a commander’s order. He obeyed without any objections.

***

The doorbell woke him. He heard his mother's footsteps in the corridor, and then recognized the voice of Sinan Bey. According to his watch it was almost nine o'clock. The smell of grilled sausage reminded him that he had invited his old friend for breakfast.

He jumped out of bed immediately, went into the bathroom. A couple of minutes later, he joined Sinan Bey and her mother at the kitchen table.

“But you're in your pajamas!” yelled the outraged mother.

Sinan Bey made a gesture with his hand to calm her:

“It's okay madam. We have already seen each other several times in pajamas in the dorms, during our college years.

But Mrs. Alpergun was not happy.

“But now he is a diplomat, he speaks three languages, he goes to the balls in the salons of embassies and he meets important people.”

Hayri pulled a chair near Sinan Bey who put his arm on the shoulder.

"Do not worry Hanimefendi[29]. Hayri and I are old acquaintances", he said with a smile.

Then turned to his friend:

"How is your neck?"

Hayri slightly lowered his head to say "yes". Yet he knew that his friend was interested in something other than the pain in the neck. He wanted to know if Hayri had nightmares. But it wasn't a question to ask in the presence of a worried mother.

"My neck is OK and I slept well," he said, to comfort him.

Actually, he was not lying, but his friend did not seem satisfied. Something important was missing in this response. He also wanted to know if Hayri had taken a sleeping pill or not. Hayri pretended not to notice this quizzical look and turned his head to his mother, as far as his brace allowed him.

"Mom? These sausages, are they coming?"

***

Half an hour after Sinan Bey had left, a driver brought the binders sent by Mrs. Consul. Hayri had never met this man before. He asked where Ahmet is. It seemed that Ahmet would be on leave for an indefinite period.

He put the files on the desk in his room. Normally, he would open them immediately and begin to examine. But now, he wanted to do something else.

---

[29] Hanimefendi (Turkish): Lady.

A look out the window was enough for him to make his decision. It was beautiful.

“I'll go for a walk,” he said.

An idea which did not please his mother.

“With what you have around your neck? Isn’t it dangerous? Did your doctor give the permission do that? Watch out for cars when you cross the streets.”

To avoid this deluge of maternal recommendations, he had to get out as soon as possible. He rushed into his room and began to dress.

The phone rang. His mother answered. He heard a conversation in Turkish. Who was she talking to?

“Hayri! It's Arda. He wants to talk to you.”

Arda was an old friend from high school. Hayri did not have the opportunity to see him for at least a decade. He was living in Paris and someone had probably talked to him about the accident.

He went into the living room and grabbed the phone. Arda was calling to invite him for a dinner tonight. A group of friends would be getting together in a Turkish restaurant. Hayri accepted the invitation. After the hospital days, he needed that. Apparently Arda knew nothing of the accident. Actually, none of his friends in Paris was aware. His ‘collar’ would make a sensation.

“I'll be late tonight,” he told to his mother. “I am going to have dinner with friends.”

She looked sad. His son was not a little boy and was no more obedient to her.

However, she was aware of her luck. Living with her son was a rare favor for a mother who gets old. She could be left alone in Turkey. His son had been kind enough to bring her with him to France.

She concluded that it was better to leave him alone for tonight.

“Okay. When you get back, I'll probably be in bed, she said.”

“Don’t worry mom. I will be quite.”

***

Once in the street, Hayri felt very happy. An autumn breeze brushed his cheek, reminding him that he had failed to take his overcoat. “Too bad,” he said, and walked quickly to keep warm. There was no way to return home for the overcoat.

He always loved walking. It was a good exercise for the body. And for the brain as well. He could think when walking, especially when walking alone. When he was kid, didn’t he develop all his best ideas when walking?

But now, he was no longer that young. He did not need to create ideas. He had already played almost all his cards. Now, all he needed was a quiet life; with no woman other than his mother, and no children other than the one in his memories.

Thinking deeply and walking at the same time might have some drawbacks. He was not paying attention where he was going. Maybe that was the reason why Rodin had sculpted the Thinker in sitting position.

He was surprised to find himself at the entrance to the 'Jardin du Luxembourg[30]'. He paused a moment watching the photos hung on the fence. But walking down the rue de Médicis was not really what he wanted to do. Visiting the Garden seemed more interesting. The visit of the outdoor photo exposition would be for another time.

He no longer felt the cold. The sun had begun to make him feel the heat. He began to walk down the aisle, slowly. This was the first time he was coming here since his arrival to Paris. His last visit was long time ago, when he was only thirteen. He had lots of memories here.

Arriving at the pool in front of the Palace, he stopped and looked around. Nothing had changed since his childhood. But why would it change? This wasn't Turkey, this was France.

Something, may be a memory, pushed him towards the Edmond Rostand Square. He exited the Garden from another gate. Once there, he stopped and looked around him. He might be taken for a tourist.

But he was not a tourist. Just a solitary walker with his reveries, with a brace around the neck

The view of the McDonald's opposite the fountain, spoiled a little the nostalgia. When he was thirteen, it was not there. His lips mimicked the lyrics of and old song:

Those were the days, my friend.

What would he do, exactly? Walk down the Boulevard St. Michel towards the river or go somewhere else?

---

[30] Luxembourg Garden

He looked at his watch. It was almost half past twelve. Dinner at Turkish restaurant was scheduled for seven o'clock. So he had more than six hours to kill.

To kill time? In Paris it is a crime to kill time. Instead, we let it live.

Someone he met somewhere, had said that. But who was he? He could not remember.

The billboard of a bus caught his eye. He read: *Aladdin and the Wonderful Lamp.* It was an animated film. A film he had seen when he was a child. Would he watch it, again?

Off course not! The idea of going to a movie was not good one and wouldn't that be just another way of 'killing time'? He had to find something interesting but not criminal.

Finally something came to his mind. He would visit his genius friend! The 'genie' of the magic lamps.

He could go the store of his friend Arda. Certainly they would have dinner together tonight, but he always wanted to see his store. However, he needed the exact address. A search of his pockets gave no result. He had left the address book at home. The one that he had carefully updated before his departure for Paris. And he still had no cell phone.

He began looking for a phone booth to call his mother so that she finds his address book to ask her the address.

Along the way he saw a sign: *Internet Garden*, which suggested him another idea. He entered immediately. A little search in Google revealed to him the address.

The store was in the 10th quarter[31]. He decided to go on foot. That could be nicer than taking the subway or the bus.

After a walk of half an hour, he arrived to his destination. He read the store name on the sign that seemed to come straight from the nineteenth century:

City of Light - old lighting

He walked slowly and peered through the window. His buddy, recognizable despite his beard, was sitting behind a table, reading a great book.

A bell hanging on the door, announcing his entry. His old friend gave him a curious look above his reading glasses.

"Good morning monsieur. How are you doing?" said Hayri, with an engaging smile.

Her old friend did not recognize him at once. However, Hayri believed that his own face had not changed too much. How many years were passed since the last time they had seen each other? Ten, twelve? ...

He decided to make a farce:

"Do you also fix rechargeable flashlights, monsieur?" he said, unable to keep himself from laughing.

So, Arda recognized him. Later he would tell that it was his voice that had betrayed.

"Hayri!" he said. "What a nice surprise!"

They conversed for over an hour. They talked about their high school memories and their life after school.

[31] Arrondissement (of Paris): Borough.

The store of Arda was full of antique lamps, oil, and gas. They were all priceless. One had to watch every movement of his body not to break any of these objects.

His friend explained how each of these lamps worked and promised him a demonstration for his next visit.

When he quitted the shop, he felt like a different man. He has the privilege to know such a man, a man who was a world authority in his field.

***

Arriving at the restaurant, he took a glance at his watch. The appointment was set for 7pm and it was almost time. He entered. Arda was not there yet. As usual, he had arrived before anyone else. Many people loved to make his friends wait but Hayri was always ahead.

He walked out quickly pretending not to hear the waitress calling him "monsieur?" Spending fifteen minutes through the streets and making some window shopping looked like a good idea.

He foolishly wandered around the restaurant and of course he got lost. He quickened his pace, passed through the same streets several times. He was drenched in sweat when he finally found his way.

The waitress led him to a table at the back of the restaurant. Five people were already sitting. Three women and two men. With his arrival, the genders were in balance. Mehmet Bey, head of the organization, had thought of everything. Three men and three women. Arda introduced his wife. Mehmet Bey presented a young woman, saying she was his fiancée. Hayri had already heard about the young “fiancées” of Mehmet Bey. She did not look very smart with her makeup of prima donna.

The third woman introduced herself:

“My name is Esther,” she said. “I am German.”

“I could have guessed that,” thought Hayri, shaking her hand.

“How do you do?” he said, without saying his own name, in return.

“No need to be polite,” he thought. He would play the bad diplomat tonight.

Questions about his brace came immediately. He spoke of the accident, without giving details. Everyone spoke French. But sometimes the conversation turned to English.

After a few moments Hayri felt the stares of the German lady.

“Do you like Racine[32]?” she asked.

But what a writer of tragedy had to do at that table? Ah! So, she was an intellectual. He would like to say: “Racine? Oh, yes, I know. This is the name of my neighbor's canary.”

But he has already been a rude a moment ago, by not saying his name. So he chose to say:

“Yes, why?”

“I have two tickets for ‘Ester’ at Palais-Royal[33] for Thursday night. Would you like to come? This is tragedy of Racine,” she said.

[32] Racine: French tragedy writer, 17th century.
[33] Théâtre du Palais-Royal: Theater of Palais Royal

Dinner passed with typical intellectual conversations. They talked about Molière, Sartre, sex, AIDS, French cuisine, strange Americans and global economy.

The "fiancée" of Mehmet Bey wanted to ask a question. Hayri, curious, listened carefully.

"Why is it always the woman who works in Turkey, while men do nothing?"

She should be dumber than she looked. Hayri, under the influence of alcohol, tried to laugh:

"Because it is through the hard work that they can keep in shape," said Hayri. "Otherwise, they would get fat and their husbands won't like them anymore. And they would take a second wife, or a third, maybe a fourth."

She did not understand the sarcasm.

"What a horror! But instead of working hard like that, to keep their shape, they could go to the gym."

Towards the end of the evening, they were all drunk. The last topic was the expressions: being drunk like a Polish, Turkish head[34], strong as a Turk, staying French[35], handsome as a god, building castles in Spain, speaking French as a Spanish cow[36], etc. And they laughed a lot. Ah, intellectuals! As usual, they were incurable.

When he returned home his mom was sleeping. He went to bed immediately and closed his eyes.

"Oh! Zut[37]!" he said in French. I didn't take my pill."

---

[34] Tête de Turc (Turkish head): Escape goat (French expression).

[35] Staying French: Being (or staying) away from the subject matter (Turkish expression).

[36] Speaking French very badly. (French expression).

But he was too lazy to stand up.

***

It did not take too long to realize that he was in a dream.

Before him, lay a huge flat field where the green was the dominant color. Far away, almost at the horizon, he could see the edge of a forest. The sky was gray. Rays of sun were piercing the clouds here and there, to make spots in some areas on the grass.

He wondered: "In this great scene of dream, I'm an actor or a spectator?"

To find out, he threw himself to the ground and rolled on the grass laughing like a kid. He felt happy. This was the proof that he was in a dream. There was no other way for him of being happy.

And in this dream he would be an actor. He felt that. And perhaps the protagonist…

He stood up to look around. On his left, at a distance of two hundred yards, lay a herd of deer. This was the first time he was seeing sitting dear. They were about thirty in number. The farmers must have left them free so that they can graze.

At his approach, some of the males stood up throwing him threatening looks. He slowed down his walk.

On his right was a white building in the middle of a large courtyard surrounded by high walls with the American flag flying on the roof. This was the residence of the Ambassador of Uncle Sam.

---

[37] Zut! (French): Heck!

And always to the right, a little further back, he could see the giant cross erected on a small artificial hill.

It was a place he knew. He had been here in this huge park before, seven or eight years ago. Was this dream taking him to his past?

His hand reached for his brace. It was there for him, around his neck, to confirm that the dream was happening in the present time.

But Hayri was here to try his new boomerang. He reached into his backpack and pulled it out of its holster. It was a real boomerang. On the brochure, he read 'easy throw'. That's why he had chosen it. He had painted in red and white at the risk of betraying the tradition of the Aborigines. This could be a crime but this was also the only way to see it from distance on the grass.

He thought he was far enough from everything that he could damage with this new toy. He noticed he was under surveillance, not only by the herd, but also by the cameras mounted on the walls of the Ambassador's residence. One could be as dangerous as the other.

The park entrance was a mile from where he was standing. Would he be able to run that distance quickly in case of a deer attack? He thought he could. He had always been a good runner.

Reassured, he waved a friendly hello to the cameras of Uncle Sam, licked his finger and held it in the air to detect the wind direction. The brochure said to hold the boomerang at an angle of ten degrees from the vertical.

This would not be his first experience with this magical instrument. The first time he had seen a picture in a book, he was a child. "This must be a wonderful toy!" he had said. He even broke the window of a house with his 'homemade' boomerang. This experiment had made him understand that this was not a toy but a weapon invented by the aborigines of Australia. "But what is an aborigine?" he asked himself, before going back in the book to find out.

Finally abandoning his memories from the past, he made his first throw with the new boomerang, which ended in failure. After a short fly, it was planted in the lawn about ten meters away.

All male deer in the herd rose. Hayri stood still for a few seconds before making any move, to make sure he would not be attacked. He went to pick up the boomerang and returned to its first position for the second throw. Another lick of the index with saliva confirmed him that the wind had not change its direction.

At this moment, another herd of deer appeared at the edge of the forest. Those were the babies, running toward adults. There has been a ripple at first. Half of the deer from the adult's herd rose. The arrival of little ones had excited them.

A car noise forced Hayri to look to his right. A black limousine was rolling down the road to the Embassy building. The cameras were turned to the newcomer.

Neither the herd nor Uncle Sam were no longer paying attention to him. It was the perfect time for the second test. He threw the boomerang with all his strength. It jumped away like a falcon from his hand. After flying about twenty meters parallel to the ground, it made an ascent of ten meters like a helicopter, then began its return towards Hayri, as if sliding down an inclined plane.

The return of the boomerang was terrifying like the attack of the falcon to its prey!

He hesitated a moment. Would he try to catch it up as the brochure explained, or let it pass? The return of the boomerang could be very dangerous for the launcher.

In fact, the boomerang flew far above his head. A jump like a bad basketball player was not enough to catch it up. Like a 'spinning saw', the boomerang passed brushing his fingertips and Hayri fell on the ground on his back.

He stood up immediately. His toy landed about ten yards behind him. He rushed to pick it up. Without wasting a second he threw it again with full force.

Then again, and again ... He threw a dozen times.

Every time he threw, the boomerang obeyed by an impressive flight. But it disobeyed on its return, annoying his master.

He managed to catch it twice. There was pain on his fingers on the right hand. Why didn't he bring his gloves?

Tired, he sat on the lawn beside his bag, pulled out a bottle of water and drank half. He had never had that fun before. He was proud of himself. Proud and tired...

When he finally had the idea to check his watch, he was surprised to see it was almost 4pm. He had only half hour to catch the last bus to town.

He regretted. The abandonment of this pleasure seemed impossible. However, there was nothing to do. The walk to the bus stop would take at least fifteen minutes.

When he was about to get up, he heard a groan.

He turned his head to all sides to see where it came from. His neck, which had left him alone until now, started to give him pain.

Deer, which lay quietly on the lawn seemed totally ignoring him. The cameras of the Embassy were oriented inside the courtyard, probably towards the limo he had seen. There was no living creature nearby.

So, where the hell was that groan coming from?" Was-it perhaps only in his imagination? Was his own brain betraying him with hallucinations?

He pricked up his ears. There was no sound that anyone could hear. Even the wind had stopped blowing.

Then he remembered that he was in a dream, in a dream that seemed to blend the past and present.

He had no more desire to make a last attempt with his boomerang. He put it carefully in its case. It was time to return to the real world.

Then he heard the groan again. This time there was no mistake. It was a "real" groan.

He looked around him, shuddering. Was there a speaker hidden in the ground? Maybe someone was trying to bully him?

As a child, he had seen a film. An evil man had kidnapped a bus full of schoolchildren and buried the whole bus in a big hole he had prepared in advance. Children and the driver could only breathe through a vent pipe. Thereafter, the kidnapper had died in a car accident and no one had a clue where the kidnapped children could well be.

A shepherd had found them by chance. The poor man was very scared before understanding what was happening. Who wouldn't be afraid screams coming from the ground? But it was only in a movie.

So, he still remembered that all this was a dream. But didn't it last too long, this dream? However he should not complain, because at least this was not a nightmare. At least not yet.

He had to wake up, and fast. But how? He began walking towards the exit of the park. Passing near the cross, he heard another groan. This one sounded like a child crying.

He started to run towards the exit of the park or rather towards the end of this dream.

***

When he opened his eyes, he saw his mother standing over him.

"How are you?" she said. "I was passing near your door. I heard you moaning."

"I moaned?" asked Hayri.

"Yes, you did."

"Really?"

She stroked his cheek.

"Were you crying for your daughter, my son?"

Hayri jumped out of bed and put his arm around her.

"No, Mom. You know that I am not capable of crying. It was only a dream."

His mother opened his eyes wide.

"Ah! Another nightmare?"

"No mom. I swear. It was only a dream, a 'real' dream.

***

"And what a dream!" he said in a low voice.

After some effort, he had managed to convince his mother to return to her bed. He had waited until she fell asleep, then he left the house.

He was still feeling the effect. It certainly was not a nightmare. He knew about the nightmares, especially since the accident.

As for the scene of the dream, he knew that too. He had already been at that park. This was many years ago. The size of this green land was impressive and there, he had played with his boomerang. He even remembered the deer, the giant cross on the hill and cameras of the Residence of the Ambassador of the United States.

But the groans, no! In the real world he had not heard anything like that. Something weird was happening to him, but what?

This Sunday morning, Paris was sunny but cold, but this time, he had taken his jacket.

He was walking without paying attention to where he was going. When finally he regained his senses, he noticed that he was near the Gare de Lyon[38] . He slowed down when passing near a café. The smell of the fresh coffee was overwhelming.

[38] Gare de Lyon: One of the main train terminal stations in Paris

"Bonjour monsieur!" said the waiter, inviting him inside.

He did not refuse and sat at a table near the window.

"A croque-monsieur[39] and a cup of tea, please," he said to the boss.

The service was fast. He cut a large piece of toasted sandwich and threw it into his mouth.

He realized he wanted to talk to someone about what he saw in his dream. "When you have a dream, you want to talk about it to someone, right?" he asked to himself.

But who could that person be? First, this should be someone who would listen attentively. This would eliminate his mother. She would panic.

This should be a person who would not make fun of him. So, this could not be Sinan Bey either. He would probably say: "Mon cher, this dream has probably been injected into your brain by your fakir-psychologist."

But of course! Nadir would listen to him. He would even be able to interpret his dream. It would still be funny to take a psychologist for a "dream interpreter" but Nadir seemed to be the only person Hayri could speak frankly.

He wanted to verify that he had his phone number. Tut! His portfolio was not in his pocket. He had forgotten it at home. How was he going to pay the breakfast he was eating now? The boss of the coffee shop was observing this 'strange' customer of Sunday morning. In the last hope, he searched the pockets of his jacket and found a bill of ten Euro. He had done well to take his jacket before leaving the house. He hailed the waiter to pay the check.

[39] The croquet-monsieur is a baked or fried boiled ham and cheese sandwich.

Leaving the café, the alarm of a parked car across the street rang with no apparent reason.

"But that's incredible, he said." He had enough.

Since his accident, all cars of Paris seemed to be equipped with this 'noise generators'. He was about to develop phobia. He walked fast to get away as soon as possible.

After twenty minutes of walking, without looking around, he found himself on the Boulevard St. Michel. For him, that neighborhood had always been the real Paris. Every time he got lost, he found himself here.

People were walking on the sidewalk. The bookstore Gibert was not yet open.

It came to his mind that he was invited to the theater for Thursday night. Ah, those intellectuals! They are incurable. This German woman he met last night at the Turkish restaurant, had invited him. He had decided to return to Gibert later to buy an edition of the book with explanations, published for high school students. He would read it before Thursday night.

"So that I don't stay French[40] during the show," he said, laughing at the paradox.

He cast a glance at the 'Greek Street'. That's how he liked to call the Rue de la Huchette where all the Greek restaurants of Paris were located. But was too early in the morning to see anyone on that street yet.

[40] Staying French (Turkish expression): To stay away from the subject matter. Not understanding what is going on.

But where was he going like that? He followed the tourists walking towards Notre Dame. The memory of an old song made him stop in the middle of the bridge. He repeated the words, watching the river Seine.

Under the bridges of Paris
When the night falls

Many of the songs that he had learned when he was a child were perhaps never sung by the young French today.

But why think about the past? The past might bring him bad memories. He wanted to get away immediately from his bad memories and return to the present. He looked at the Seine, water was flowing under the bridge foolishly.

So, what was this man -who is now in a coma- had thrown before getting crushed by the car he was in? Did he really wanted to be killed? How weird way to commit suicide? Hayri would probably use a gun to kill himself.

But, what kind of idea was it now? He had never thought of committing suicide. Even when he was informed that his wife was cheating on him.

Bad memories again! ...

He looked at his watch. Maybe the Gibert was open. He started to walk up the Boulevard.

Arriving at the bookstore, he saw the doors opened. Vendors were bringing the occasion books to sidewalk displays. He entered and climbed stairs. He should not look to any other book other than he was supposed to buy. Otherwise, he would not control his incurable disease to buy one or two more books. At home, more than a half dozen of books were waiting to be read.

He had no difficulty in finding what he was looking for. It was a slim booklet for students, with explanations.

"Easy to read," he thought.

On leaving, he had the idea to go to a park and start turning the pages.

Following a group of American tourists, he crossed the bridge. The steps in front of Notre Dame could be used as a seat. He did not even bother to clean the dirt.

He watched the tourists for a few minutes. Each of them had a camera. He tried to calculate the number of images of Notre Dame that were taken per day, per week and per year. Finding that it was stupid thing to do, he abandoned his calculations but continued to observe the tourists.

Then began to turn the pages, without reading. Passersby would probably think he was consulting a guide to Paris.

"I must look funny," he thought.

He remembered the words of a French friend:

"There are three Paris," he had said. "The Paris of Parisians, the Paris of tourists and the Paris of Americans."

"Americans? But what differs them from the other tourists?" had he asked.

"They are Americans, that's all," had replied his friend, with a laugh.

The French had their own weird way to observe other nations.

Fifteen minutes later, he decided that this was not a place for him. He wasn't belonging to any of these groups. There was nothing exciting for him here. He got up and cleaned his pants with his hand, trying to chase the dust. His seat was not comfortable at all. He had sore in bottom.

He wanted to do something exciting. But the exciting things could not be done during the day. He had to wait for the night. "What to do now?" he asked himself.

And the devil whispered him an idea...

***

As he rode the subway without consulting the plan, he got off one station before reaching his destination. For the rest of this way, he had go by foot now.

He walked slowly for about ten minutes, with hesitant steps. Finally he saw the Seine, and the bridge on the left. The Bridge on which his father was murdered.

He could not get closer, he preferred to look from distance. This was certainly not the exciting thing he was looking for but he was still happy to have finally come this place he had always been afraid to come. This was a kind of taboo that was demolishing now. A taboo that was perhaps the cause of his nightmares. In the next session, he would tell Nadir what he had done and how brave he had been.

He tried to cry again, without success.

V

Say: He is Allah, the One and Only
(Qur'an, Surah Al-Ikhlas 112)

God of Muslims

When the 'réveil[41]', worthy of its name, awoke Hayri, it was exactly 8 am. He stood up immediately. A slight dizziness forced him to stand at the bedside. It must be the effect of the sleeping pill. Regained his balance, he rushed into the bathroom, avoiding to be seen barefoot by his mother. He didn't want to be scolded.

[41] Réveil (Fr): alarm clock.Comes from réveiller (wake-up)

He threw a furtive glance at the sullen-looking man in the mirror. The sound of electric razor drowned the voice of his mother calling. She was announcing the breakfast. He pretended not to hear. This was a game he liked to play with his mother, since his childhood.

It was Monday and he never liked Mondays. Even when he didn't have to go to work. He remembered a story he heard in elementary school: A little boy, who was not yet old enough to go to school, hated Mondays. His older brother and his father were leaving him at home with his mother. One day his father brought him a puppy. The family decided to give the dog the name 'Monday'. Then the boy stopped hating the first day of the week. This small memory was enough to make the sullen man in the mirror smile.

His mother knocked on the door:

"Bonjour!" Breakfast is served.

Ah! How good it was to live with his mother. He could not even miss a breakfast.

***

After the breakfast, he finally decided to open the package sent from the office. It was waiting on the table in the dining room. He got surprised to find a BlackBerry instead of an ordinary mobile phone. It was even ready to operate. To make sure, he made a test by dialing the house phone. The ring brought his mother. It was really working! He made fun with his mother, who returned to the kitchen a little annoyed.

Why not give it another try? It could for example call Nadir. His card was in his wallet in his room. He got up to get it.

When walking in the corridor, he heard a strange tone. It took him a few seconds to realize that it was the BlackBerry. He returned to the room. His mother was already there.

“What is it?” she asked.

“This must be the BlackBerry, Mom.”

“The.., what?”

“My new mobile phone. Given to me by my job.”

“It has a weird tone,” she said.

Hayri took it in hand. Which button should he press to get the call? He figured it out with not much effort.

“Hello?”

“Good morning mon cher,” replied a deep voice.

Who could that be other than Sinan Bey?

“How do you know I have a mobile phone and how do you know my number that even I don’t know?”

“Aren’t you supposed to say good morning first? And how could you ever forget that ‘knowing’ is my job?”

“Oh, yes, good morning. Excuse me. I just woke up and.”

Sinan Bey cut him.

“Did you have any nightmares, last night?”

“Oh, no! Not at all. I slept very well.”

Should he change the subject quickly before Sinan Bey starts asking questions about the sleeping pills?

"I leave in an hour to go to the hospital. The doctor will probably take remove my brace. I do not think I need it anymore."

"Okay, said Sinan Bey. I called you because tonight I am going to Pideci[42] in Saint-Denis, with two friends. You know one of them. You are old acquaintances."

"Really? Who is it?"

"It will be a surprise. You would not guess. Try to be there at 7pm."

"Okay," said Hayri before hanging up.

Having listened to the conversation, his mother asked:

"So, you are not going to be home for dinner?"

She looked sad.

"Sorry mom. This is an invitation I can't refuse."

"But you must rest. You go out every night."

Hayri waved his hand to silence her. He returned to his room to find the phone number of Nadir. He felt bad for being rude to his mother, but sometimes it was the only way to stop her talking.

He dialed the number from the Blackberry. An answering machine began to speak to him, first in French, then in English. He was supposed to leave a message. But he always hated the answering machines. He hung up. Before redialing the same number, he practiced his words silently. Finally he

[42] Pideci: Turkish restaurant specialized in Pide (Food made with flour. Kind of pizza)

managed to record a message to say that he wanted to visit this afternoon Dr. Udayasekaran, at three o'clock and he would call him back to confirm.

After putting his clothes on, he headed for the door. His mother shouted from the kitchen.

“Are you leaving already?”

“I am going to the hospital, mom. They will take my brace off.

“You want me to come with you?”

“No, mom!”

***

Once on the street, Hayri called the hospital to ask if they could change the appointment to afternoon, just before his meeting with Nadir. This would be more convenient for him. But did Nadir get the message he left?

“Well, if not, it will be for another day,” he said to himself.

He looked at his watch and realized that he left home much too early. But why to complain when there is time for a walk in Paris, even early in the morning? The streets were full of Parisians in hurry. They all looked strange. Unlike him, they had specific goals. They were going to specific places, planned in advance. Mostly to their job. They looked like ants. Normally, Hayri would be nothing but one of them. But today, it was different.

He found himself by the Seine, near the Pont des Arts. At this hour, there was nobody yet on this foot-bridge. A tourist boat, full of Japanese tourists, passed under the bridge. They were shooting either side of the river with their cameras. They must have woken up very early to be in the boat at this hour.

He took the stairs down to the banks of the Seine and finally decided to sit on the bottom step. The gray waters of the river now running a few steps from him.

At this hour nothing was romantic. The wind brushed his face reminding him something from his childhood. But the memory went as quickly as it came. It was not the time to think about his childhood. He would have plenty of time later, especially if Nadir agreed to see him this afternoon.

Feeling the cold breeze, he thrust his hands into his pockets. Then he found the book, the book of Racine titled 'Ester'. The book that he had bought recently from Gibert.

***

"The doctor will be with you in a moment," said the nurse who took off the brace, leaving him alone in the office of the doctor.

Hayri looked around. It did not look like a regular hospital room. The walls were full of pictures. His doctor, was he also a painter?

He stood up to watch closely. They were all from Russian artists. He recognized the 'Uzbek Boy' by Kuzma Petrov-Vodkin. He had seen this painting at the cover of a book. None were printed. They were real reproductions on canvas, copied by a talented artist.

Hayri did not hear the door opening.

"Those reproductions are from my daughter."

This was the doctor who was speaking.

“She is a student at the School of Fine Arts in Besançon[43],” he said.

Hayri had a moment of bitterness. He thought of his own daughter. He remembered how much she liked painting. And then he thought of his wife, the famous lawyer. Her angel face appeared for a moment before his eyes.

He wanted to get away from his thoughts, immediately.

“Does your daughter lives in Besançon? Is not the city where the story of Julien Sorel's was set?”

“Oh yes. I can see that you read *Le Rouge et le Noir*[44]. I was born in Besançon, my wife too. We still have friends there, so I have no worries about my daughter. Do you know what they call people of Besançon?”

Hayri shrugged his shoulders. He did not fail to say ‘bah’ either, like a typical French gentleman.

“Bisontins and Bisontines,” said the doctor, to answer his own question.

“But this reminds me of Byzantium,” Hayri said with surprise.

“Doesn’t-it?” said the doctor, smiling.

Then he showed him a chair to sit on. Hayri obeyed. He examined his neck carefully. He told him to turn his head in several directions and asked if he feels any pain.

Hayri did not feel any pain, at least not too much. And he definitely did not want this ‘collar’ around his neck.

---

[43] A city near the border of Switzerland.

[44] The Red and The Black: historical novel of Stendhal.

The doctor was satisfied.

“Well, I can see that you are physically in good shape. Do you continue to see Dr. Udayasekaran?”

“Yes. I am planning to see him again this afternoon.”

Then, he had the idea of asking how ‘the man in a coma’ was doing?

The doctor took the question very naturally:

“He woke up yesterday for a few minutes. He even mentioned the name of his girlfriend, but went back to sleep right away. His skull injury is our main concern. Surgeons think it is wiser not to touch, for now. We'll see.”

“Do you know his identity?”

“Yes, yes. He is identified now. But I do not remember his name.”

Then he looked Hayri, straight in the eye.

“Would you like to pay him a visit?”

Hayri looked perplexed.

“I do not insist, but if you're interested, I could immediately arrange a tour for you.”

Hayri nodded his head to say “yes”.

They went out together, marched through the corridors and arrived at the elevator.

“We had moved him to a private room for security reasons. It seems that it is no longer necessary, but since his status is still delicate, we do not want to move him.”

Then he pressed button for the second floor.

They finally arrived to room 234. The chair near the door was empty and there was no policeman in sight.

Before entering, the doctor touched his arm to slow him down.

"We must be silent. This is a room transformed for patients who need special treatment."

The room was occupied with only one bed surrounded by several electronic equipment emitting regular beeps and whistles. The curtains of the window were closed. Once his eyes accustomed to the darkness, Hayri could see the body in the bed. The man was unrecognizable. His head was bandaged like a turban of a nomad and an oxygen tube was in his mouth. Even his closest friends would not have known who he was. You could still see the deep-lidded eyes that were closed. He was thin and brown. He seemed quite tall, probably taller than Hayri.

A nurse entered. She spoke to the doctor in a low voice. Hayri heard nothing. Then the doctor made a sign to Hayri and they left the room together.

"Is he going to survive?"

"In such cases, it is not easy to predict. But you never know," said the doctor.

"Who is it that pays the costs of the hospital?"

The doctor gave him a surprised look. Was Hayri asking a question that was not supposed to be asked? Maybe an explanation was necessary:

"I mean, does he need financial help? Maybe I could..."

He paused. He was talking nonsense. Why would he help a man he didn't know? And by what right? Such proposals could be made in Turkey and in some other Oriental countries. But here, it looked weird. A Western materialist would never understand that. Fortunately, the doctor was old enough to tolerate this kind of things.

"It's very generous of you," he said. "But I do not think it's necessary. He is a member of a club or an international organization of which I can't remember the name. I think the head office is in Beirut."

Then he gave him an amused look:

"Don't you worry, everything is paid."

He heard a light sound of vibration. It was doctor's pager. After casting a glance at the small device attached to his belt, he said:

"I have to leave. I am expected in an emergency meeting at the fourth floor. Can you find your way? Do not hesitate to call me if your pain comes back."

Then, he stated to walk towards the elevator. He stopped at the midway and returned to tell him:

"You are going to see Dr. Nadir, don't you? So, you can go through the skywalk."

This idea pleased Hayri. He looked at his watch. He had fifteen minutes to his appointment with Nadir.

***

Third session

"How are you doing?" asked Nadir.

"I had a dream."

"A dream? Just a dream? Not a nightmare?"

Hayri took deep breath.

"It started as a beautiful dream. But towards the end it took a strange course."

"Did you take a sleeping pill before sleeping?"

Hayri shook his head. The doctor looked at him silently for a moments then showed him the inclined chair. Hayri obeyed and laid down.

"Okay. Tell me about this dream!" said Nadir.

Hayri told him everything: the big park, the lawn, the deer, the cameras of Uncle Sam and his game with the boomerang.

"It seems you had a dream a rather too long. Dreams are short in general. This looks like an illusion, even a hallucination. Are you sure you did not take anything else?"

"Nothing."

"Recreational or street drugs either?"

Hayri felt offended.

“I do not do drugs, monsieur! Never!”

“Okay. Do not get excited. This is routine question I ask my patients.”

The doctor sat at his desk and start looking pages of a book.

“No alcohol, either?”

“I was at dinner with friends. I may have drank some raki[45]. Do you think this might be the reason?”

Nadir gestured with his hand to stop him.

“Tell me about the end of your dream.”

Hayri told him about the groans:

“I did not understand where they were coming from, he said. I could not turn my head to see what it was. I could not even run, my shoes were made of lead.

“So you could not turn your head?”

“Because of the brace on my neck.”

“Ah! So you had your neck brace, in your dream?”

It seemed silly, but it was necessary to explain a little.

“I've been in that park a couple of years ago. I recognized it in my dream. It was the ‘Phoenix Park’ in Dublin, Ireland. The largest park in Europe. I have already experienced everything that I saw at the beginning of my dream.”

He paused. Nadir asked:

“And all of a sudden, you heard someone moaning?”

[45] Raki: Popular alcoholic drink (strong) in Turkey.

"Yes."

"And you started to run?"

Hayri made nodded his head.

There has been a silence. Nadir rose slowly from his chair. He walked for a while in the room. Hayri was watching him.

Doctor stopped all of a sudden. He had a strange a strange look on his face. Then he asked:

"And you came here to me, expecting I interpret this dream of yours?"

He looked offended. Hayri tried to speak calmly to avoid stuttering.

"Mr. Udayasekaran, this is not the purpose of my visit. This dream made me realize that there is something in my head. Something I can't define."

He tried to smile and say something to amuse.

"My brain is like being haunted by a ginny. Don't you think I should do something to get it out of there? This is reason I came to you."

Nadir's look was still serious.

"Like the ginny of Aladdin's lamp?" he asked in a sarcastic tone.

Hayri remained silent. Nadir spoke:

"Okay," he said. "But on one condition. You will promise to come to my psychotherapy sessions regularly."

Like a wise and obedient child, Hayri nodded his head, which caused him a slight pain.

“Your dream, I will interpret it, but later. You will now continue to tell me more about your adventures. What was the name of this city of eastern Anatolia?”

“Diyarbakir,” said Hayri.

Then he added:

“It is also known as the city of scorpions.”

“Really?” said Nadir, surprised.

“I've already told you all of my adventures in Diyarbakir. One day in June, which was the last day of school, my father came back home with an important news. He was assigned to a position at the Ministry of Foreign Affairs. In two weeks we would go to Ankara.”

“Did this make you happy?”

“We were all happy. I was jumping all around the house. We immediately began to do pack. And two weeks later we were at the station. Many people that we had met during our stay in Diyarbakir, had come to say goodbye to us. I've never encountered elsewhere such friendly people.”

Nadir smiled. Hayri was kind of a man who saw no objection to show his feelings. “He would never make a good poker player,” he thought.

“Among our friends who came to the station, there was someone. I was surprised to see him. It was Rashad, one of the big boys at school. One of the two boys who had saved my life. He also had come to say goodbye. He told me that after he had been expelled from the school, he had gone to live with his uncle in a small town north of Diyarbakir. I asked him how he knew I was leaving today. He told me:

"There is a small bird in your head. He flew to my home to tell me that you're leaving."

"A little bird in the head? It's interesting," said Nadir.

"He said he would still take the exams to finish the school."

"This means he is brave man," said Nadir.

"Yes. That day I admired him. He also said something that surprised me a lot."

"What did he say?"

Hayri savored the pleasure of seeing the great curiosity on the doctor's face. At this point, he was at his merci. It was obvious that the doctor would die to know the rest of his story. So he decided to take his time.

"May I have some water, please? I am thirsty."

He was lying. He had no desire at all. Ah, that was wicked!

Nadir took a bottle of Evian from a small refrigerator and handed him along with a glass. Hayri poured a little water. He watched at the same time the expressions on the face of the doctor. It should not extend the game because he could lose interest.

"He told me we would meet again, some years later."

He looked Nadir to see his reaction. But the doctor remained unmoved. Hayri continued to speak:

"At that moment, I did not take these words seriously. It seemed impossible, but we met anyway."

"How?"

Hayri was pleased to see the curiosity again on his face. But this time, he would not torture him.

"Several years later, in Istanbul, at the French Catholic High School. And later in Ankara, at the university. We even shared the room at residences of the university."

"What a coincidence," said Nadir, surprised. "But you'll be telling me your academic adventures later. I would first like to know what happened after you left Diyarbakir. You came to France, right?"

"Yes. Two years after arriving in Ankara, one evening my father told us that he had news: we were going to France!"

"What was your reaction?"

"Difficult to describe. My mother was silent."

"And you?"

"I was excited. But also worried. I was thirteen."

"For how long your stay in France was planned?

"Three years or more. But something happened the second year."

Nadir stopped him with hand gesture.

"I know what happened. It must be difficult to talk about it. We will come back to this later. Will you now tell me your first days in France? What was your impressions? Have you had a cultural shock?"

“I wouldn’t say a shock, but there was a lot of different things. First, I took a course to learn a few words of French, before going to school. It was an audio-visual course that helped me a lot.

“Did you get yourself friends easily?”

“Yes. Thank to soccer. I still wasn’t a great player, but every time they missed one in their team, they came to get me.”

“Did you have many conversations with them?”

“Rarely. But sometimes we boys, we talked among ourselves. We were talking about girls, soccer, even serious things.”

“Serious things? Such as?”

“Since they were speaking so fast, I wasn’t understanding most of the words.”

He paused. Nadir’s face was full of curiosity. For the first time in his life, Hayri had found a person listening to him carefully, with patience. He had already told him many things about himself and was ready to say even more.

“One day after a soccer game, we sat down. They were still talking among themselves. I was understanding some of the words. All of a sudden I realized that I was the subject of their conversations. Shortly after, one of them turned to me. It was the other called ‘Gaillard[46]’. I never knew if that was his real name. He paused me a question:

“You're Muslim, right?”

“I nodded my head.”

[46] Gaillard (Fr): Robust, strong

"What is ala?"

"It took me a few seconds to realize he was trying to say 'Allah'. I didn't know how to answer this question and I remained silent for a moment. During my silence, they exchanged a few words with each other. Then another one, who thought he knew the answer, asked me to check: *"He is God of Muslims, right?"*

"I was shocked. I tried to explain him with my broken French: *But isn't there only one God? And is he not the same God for all the believers in the world?*"

A bitter smile appeared on the face of Nadir.

"So, did you feel yourself different from others?"

Yes. This is exactly what Hayri had felt and he would always be 'different'. Later, after he returned home, he had checked in the French dictionary for the word 'God' and had learned that the word God in French does not take an article[47].

He looked at his watch. Nadir noticing his gesture, asked:

"Are you tired? Do you want to continue tomorrow?"

Hayri had told about everything of his childhood 'adventures' in France. There were only two things to say. It might be necessary to tell them now, rather than leaving them for tomorrow.

"A year had passed. I had learned French pretty well. One day, out of the school, one of my friends suggested me to walk home instead of taking the bus. His house was near ours. Like me, he was one of the guys who was

[47] Article *'le'* (the) is not used with the word *Dieu* (God)

silent in class. He always wore a small cross at the end of a chain around his neck. He said he was curious about one thing. He asked me if I was circumcised. Then he wanted to know the details of the 'operation' and if I had pain. I told him that it hurt me a lot. Then I explained the details of the circumcision. The poor guy started making faces. Looked like he was the one in pain. Of course, I was exaggerating a little bit, but it amused me."

Nadir smiled.

"Then he asked me a question that shocked me," said Hayri.

"What?"

"He told me that he had read in a newspaper that circumcised men take less pleasure when having sex."

"That, you can't know, because you can't compare both cases," said Nadir. "Do you regret being circumcised?"

"No. They say circumcision also has some advantages. I heard that the majority of Americans do that."

There has been a couple seconds of silence. This was rather a weird conversation. Hayri wished to change the subject.

"This does not look to be the reason for your nightmares, does-it?" asked Nadir.

"No. I don't think so," said Hayri.

This is what Nadir was trying to find out. The 'thing' that was haunting his patient in nightmares.

"So, shall we continue?"

He told his story with the dog and how he was afraid. Nadir had a wide smile on his face when Hayri finished his story.

“This dog, do you think he is the reason of your nightmares?”

“Oh, no. I don’t think so. I had forgotten all about it the same day.”

“So, you are no longer afraid of dogs?

“Sometimes,” said Hayri with a smile. “When I see one on the street, I switch sidewalks.”

Nadir was thinking again. Then he spoke:

“Good. So finally, are you ready today to tell me about the murder of your father?”

Voilà! The most difficult moment had arrived. He could postpone it until tomorrow or to another day. But he chose to do it. He felt he could do it now. Maybe tomorrow, he wouldn’t have the courage to talk about it at all.

Then he told to his doctor everything:

“I was surprised when I arrived home. There were some people. People I haven’t met before. They said they were coming from the Turkish Embassy. My mother was lying on the couch, unconscious. For a moment I thought she was dead.”

He sighed for a moment. Oh, God! It was so difficult to talk about this, despite all those years that have passed. Nadir gave him an encouraging smile. He was listening carefully. Hayri continued:

“They told me that there had been an attack to Embassy’s car, on the bridge.”

***

The sun had already set down and the cold air had begun to be felt.

Hayri was walking, hands stuffed in the pockets of his jacket. He was walking fast, without paying attention to anything around him. He was trying to clear his thoughts, in vain. The last words of Nadir didn't stopped making endless echoes in his brain:

"That way, we will not get anywhere," he had said. He was not able to find the real cause of the problem. Contrary to what he thought at first, the cause was not the murder of his father. So, if it wasn't the assassination of his father what could that thing be? The 'thing' that kept following Hayri behind in nightmares.

Maybe he was wrong. Maybe the famous psychologist was looking for a reason that did not exist at all. But what was most 'funny', he had offered to do a test. He did not want Hayri take sleeping pills tonight. If he was healed, that is to say, if the assassination of his father was the only reason behind these nightmares, he would be able to sleep peacefully.

"If not, we'll see," he had said.

"Why not to try?" had thought Hayri. What did he have to lose? So he had agreed.

And he remembered the last question that Nadir asked, just before leaving his office. The question had made him blush. The doctor had asked: "At what age did you have your first masturbation?"

This was too much!

***

This was not the Saturday evening but still at the Turkish restaurant Pideci, almost all the tables were occupied. The salon was full of smoke despite a poster of a little boy holding a sign: ‘Please do not smoke.’

Hayri looked around and saw Sinan Bey making him sign. He was sitting on at a table with two men.

He joined them. They shook hands. Neither of the two other men looked familiar. One of them was about ten years older than everybody else. The other was completely bald, with a mustache too big for his face.

“Do you know Kemal?” asked Sinan Bey.

Hayri tried to figure out which one of them was Kemal. He had even known a ‘Kemal’ in his life?

“Do you remember me? Asked the bald man with big moustache. In college, we took together the course 'Symbolic Logic'.”

He kept touching his mustache. Speaking of 'Symbolic Logic', Hayri and this man were certainly not in the same Venn diagram.

“Is that so?” said Hayri, trying to give an interested look.

“I was seeing you often with a girl. She was beautiful,” he said.

The evening was not promising to be a pleasant one. It was true that Aysel was beautiful, very beautiful. Even too much.

“I failed the exam, I had to take this course for a second time,” continued the man.

“I was about to fail too,” said Hayri. “I have got just a C.”

"Where did you make your military service?" asked the older man. Hayri still did not know his name.

"I was in the Navy, instructor in the School of Junior Officers," he answered.

"Oh, lucky you!" said the man. "Life is easy in the Navy. There is nothing but fun."

Hayri had no desire to contradict him. Besides, the man continued to speak without really awaiting any response.

"I was in the military patrol station, in the eastern Anatolia. Those were the years when the terrorists walked freely in the mountains. The government was struggling to establish its authority."

He was talking non-stop. He talked about the battles with terrorists, the hardships of the mountain life. In the East, one could not trust anybody. Some of the local people and peasants were helping soldiers, but others were shooting them in the back.

Even Sinan Bey did not interrupt him. This was starting to be annoying to Hayri. He had come here hoping to relax a bit. Fortunately their meal arrived promptly and the talkative man started to eat like a hungry lion.

It was a unique opportunity to start the conversation with Kemal.

"I remember having seen you in class Symbolic Logic (he was lying). But did we meet later?"

"No, said Kemal. My family had financial problems. I had to interrupt my studies for a few years."

"Ah. That explains why I haven't seen you later," said Hayri.

He thought it would be wise not to ask him if he had his degree.

Everyone was eating quickly. Apparently dinner would last half an hour at most. Hayri tried to restart the conversation:

"The streets were full of tourists today. I did not know it was the season."

"I made the same observation," said Kemal. "The majority were American tourists".

"Ah, tourists!" said the other man. "But I know about 'tourists'."

He had just finished his meal and was beginning to talk.

"I met them during my military service."

"Really?" said Sinan Bey." I thought you had done your service in the eastern mountains."

"That's right, I was in the East, in pursuit of terrorists. It is where I met tourists from Europe and United States."

"What the hell they were doing at those dangerous lands?" asked Sinan Bey.

"Strange, isn't?" said the man. "Instead of enjoying the beauty of the turquoise coast of Western Anatolia, they came to see the mountains of the East. Bare mountains where forests were burned down by the government, so that the terrorists can't hide."

The looks of Hayri and Kemal met. Both, had no intention of interfering in this conversation.

"But these 'tourists', they kept coming to those lands where there was only dust and blood. And Kurdish kids were throwing stones to their cars, just for fun."

The waiter interrupted to ask if they wanted tea or coffee. They all ordered Turkish coffee. The only thing that seemed to be common between them.

"But why on earth were they there?" exploded finally Sinan Bey. If they were the spies, why would they put their families at risk?"

This issue caused a smile of satisfaction on the face of the talkative man.

"Good question. Yes, these 'tourists' came as a family with their children and with some 'sketches' in their pockets, seeking the treasures of their grandfathers and their great mothers who had survived. Stories of treasures were told from generations to generations. Little treasures they had buried in the ground, quickly, just before leaving the country where they were born."

Those words said, there has been a silence. The people around them had heard the old man who was speaking loudly.

Hayri was uncomfortable. He was already tired and wanted to leave.

"So, did they find what they were looking for?" asked Sinan Bey.

"According to rumors, there were some 'guides' who offered their assistance and they shared the loot."

Sinan Bey waved the waiter to bring the bill. He refused to share the money and paid it all. Before separating from the other two men out, the one who was talkative told his name. It was Atila.

Sinan Bey offered Hayri to drive home, but he refused.

“But I will still accompany you to your car, he said. I would like to speak to you.”

Sinan Bey was forced to park a little further. They began to walk.

“This morning, when you told me on the phone that there would be someone tonight, I was expecting to see someone close to me.”

“Who were you expecting?” asked Sinan Bey.

“This person, Kemal, even in college, I did not see him very often. And after so many years, tonight I found him very changed: bald head, big mustache. I did not recognize him.”

Sinan Bey laughed.

“Everyone can’t have the same luck as you. What you're doing to stay young like that?

Hayri could say “I sold my soul to the devil,” but he hold his tongue. Sinan Bey was not the kind of man who could digest such jokes.

“I talked to Dr. Udayasekaran about the murder of my father,” he said suddenly.

Contrary to what he expected, Sinan Bey did not react. But he said something that startled him:

“Today, you went to see this man you hit.”

“You know that too? But how?” Hayri asked.

“Knowing is my job. So how is he doing?”

“Still in a coma.”

“Did you see his face?”

“A little, yes. Why?”

“Is he someone you know?”

“No! Why everyone keep asking me this question? I do not know him!”

“Is it possible that you've seen him long time ago?”

“But why do you say that? If I had seen him before, I would probably recognize.”

“But tonight, you did not recognize Kemal either.”

“What do you mean, Sinan Bey? I do not understand.”

They arrived near the car. Sinan Bey offered to drive him home again, but Hayri was determined to walk.

“Sinan Bey! I think there's something you're not telling me. You are a good friend. Why don't tell me what is going on?”

“I think the doctor took you by this man in a coma, to see your reaction. They want to make sure you really don't know him.”

“But why would I know? It was an accident, wasn't it?”

“I believe that the French police has some doubts about that. I think the cameras recorded you when you were doing laps around his bed.”

“Et voilà![48]” murmured Hayri. This was explaining all. He had made everyone paranoid by making a suspicious visit to the man they hit.

[48] Et voilà (Fr): There you go.

“But don’t worry, said Sinan Bey, starting the engine. They will close the file. The investigation is completed.”

It was comforting. It was not fun at all to have the cops on his back, whatever the reason.

Sinan Bey said goodnight and left.

With no rush, Hayri started to walk in the streets. He thought of the words of the talkative man:

> “*Before leaving the country where they were born.*”

VI

Victory has a thousand fathers,
but defeat is an orphan.
John F. Kennedy.

Orphan[49]

After leaving his companions at about nine o'clock, Hayri thought it was too early to go home. He took the metro to the Opera Square. He wanted to drink a hot chocolate at Café de la Paix. Arrived there, he saw that all the tables were occupied. He changed his destination. A walk to the boulevard of the Italians was more fun.

At the other side of the boulevard, a less crowded cafe caught his attention. He crossed the street and entered. A large TV screen was giving the news.

[49] "Orphan" (computer jargon): a piece of program (often undesired) that continue to operate in a computer although its associated "parent" application has been removed, uninstalled or killed.

Two men and a woman leaning on the bar were watching. All three cast a glance at the newcomer, then returned to the screen.

Hayri - having changed his mind - ordered a cappuccino. He picked a table facing the window. The view of the neon lights of the Paramount Movie Theater was amazing. His eyes froze on their flushing bright lights.

A sip of his coffee burned his tongue, but he loved it. A cappuccino was supposed to be hot, wasn't it?

He was hearing the whispers of three people at the bar, without paying attention to what they said. However, he heard the words 'terrorist' and 'explosion'. A group of journalists at TV were commenting on an assassination attempt against the First Lady of France, somewhere in the world. The terrorists had failed.

"Ah! Idiots! They missed it!" shouted the woman at the bar.

Spontaneously Hayri turned his head towards her. Their eyes met. She could not be a terrorist sympathizer. It was obvious that she was only trying to attract the attention of the newcomer.

Hayri knew that women find him good-looking. They look at him in the street, in restaurants, at work, everywhere. He used to like that, especially when he was younger.

But they were just looking at him and this was lasting only a few moments. Shortly after, they lost interest. He never knew why.

He was not a flirty in nature. He was cautious, even with 'easy' women. Those who took the initiative first, had never interested him. Shy ones were his favorite, especially those who had innocent looks. Even if they were not.

He finished his coffee, taking big gulps. Two euros left on the table would be more than sufficient. He stood up.

As he passed the bar, his eyes once again crossed the woman's eyes. With a little less makeup, she would be beautiful. Her disappointed look was telling him: “Why are you leaving so early?”

Once on the street, he looked at his watch. It was still too early to go home. He walked to the Paramount Movie Theatre and looked at the large posters. None of the films seemed interesting and he did not feel like going to the movie. Not to this one anyway. Tonight he wanted to do something crazy.

He tried to remember the name of the movie theatre that he read in the newspaper a few weeks ago. What’s the name of the town near Los Angeles where celebrities live?

“Beverly Hills!” he shouted, proud of his good memory.

Passersby gave him suspicious looks. Yes, he remembered the name, but now it was to know where it is located. The author of the article had written that the movie theatre is in the 2nd quarter. Naturally, he did not give the full address. Hayri began to wander in the streets, almost empty at this hour of the night.

The Devil helped him whenever he wanted to do something ‘bad’ and he would be faithful this time too. After walking for about ten minutes at random, he saw a small street. Would he take a look?

The pink neon poster attracted him like a mosquito.

The Beverly, which was the name of a pocket cinema, seemed welcoming. A man in his fifties, sitting at the counter, spoke to him:

“The film will start in a minute, monsieur. Hurry!”

The twelve euros paid for the ticket seemed too high. He did not fail to read the warnings on a wall:

ALL EXITS ARE FINAL
STRICTLY PROHIBITED UNDER 18

When he entered the salon the lights were still on. He was surprised to see that almost all the seats were filled and the lights went out before he found a one. Walking blindly he stepped on the foot of a man who yelled him. Finally he could sit.

A man and a woman, almost naked, were on the scene. There was even no introduction to the film. They were preparing to make love in the kitchen. They had no time to lose. Apparently, everything was beginning with sex and finishing with sex.

He tried to focus on the film that seemed quite old, form 70s or 80s. It didn’t look like the modern porn that anyone could download from the Internet. The woman in garter belts was not sexy.

People were probably coming here to kill their boredom. Maybe it was a better way than doing Sudoku alone at home. A snore coming from behind, made him smile. Couldn’t the poor man find a better spot to take a nap for twelve euros?

He could not stay longer than fifteen minutes. He got up and left the theatre.

A light rain was waiting for him in the street. "It is time to go home," he told himself. He had enough for tonight, and now all he wanted was a good sleep.

***

He put the key in the lock and turned slowly to avoid making noise. It was not the time to wake his mother, not only to disturb her sleep but also to avoid embarrassing questions.

A note taped to the door of the kitchen was waiting for him. His mother never failed to give instructions:

> *Hayri, my son,*
>
> *The daughter of Madame Hermine has given birth today, earlier than expected. Her husband is on a business trip in the United States. They have no one else to help them. Tonight, I'll stay at the hospital with them. You'll find your dinner in the fridge.*
>
> *Your mom.*

She was nice to sign "Your mom". Who else could write him such a note?

Madame Hermine was one of her mother's old friends from the French School of Sisters of Istanbul. He was not surprised to see his mother run to help her old friend.

Of course, he was not hungry. The big *pide*[50] he eaten as dinner was still heavy in his stomach. His desire to sleep had gone. One of the birds on the *bird clock* in the living room began to sing. It was indicating the midnight.

---

[50] Kind of pizza

More determined than ever not to take sleeping pills, he had to invent a hobby until his desire to sleep comes back. Watching TV was not a good idea. His mother had left Sudoku books on the coffee table in the living room but they might make him worse. He didn't like Sudoku much anyway.

On the shelf, there were few books on economics and a book about French food. None of them deserved to be read, especially after midnight.

He pulled the large drawer of the cabinet where his mother was hiding the bottle of whiskey. She had always been afraid that his son became an alcoholic, especially after the betrayal of his wife. So, she always tried to take action.

The whiskey was there. It was an Irish. He smiled with satisfaction. There was another thing next to the bottle: a photo album. He took both of them and put them on the table. Then he went to the kitchen to get a glass and ice. Of course, there was no ice in the fridge. His mother, as usual, had forgotten to put water in the strays. He would have to drink it dry. Wasn't it the usual way to drink the Irish anyway?

He returned to the bedroom and undressed. Now, he was with his underwear. This was a privilege that a man could afford himself only when his wife was not home. In this case, this would be his mother.

Tonight, he wanted to continue his little follies. Cigarette smoking could be another one. He had stopped smoking for eleven years.

Luck had always been a bit mischievous with him. The day he had stopped smoking, he had found a Dupont lighter, on a sidewalk, lost by an unlucky smoker. Throughout his life, he had the chance to have the best of everything: a special father admired and respected by everyone, a marriage with a beautiful woman, a daughter like an angel descended from heaven.

He could not keep either of them.

Small consolation, the Dupont, he could keep it always in his pocket, in his bag or on the nightstand beside his bed. He liked to play with, but it was never used to light a cigarette.

Cigarettes? There should be some in the drawer where he had taken a bottle of whiskey.

With the smoke of Gauloises Blondes in the air and the album with the photos of his daughter Seray. He made efforts for a few tears, but failed. Finally he decided to lay down on the bed. He was tired, both physically and mentally.

But the sleep did not come on so soon. Some small souvenirs continued to bug him just before he fell asleep.

This beautiful naked woman on his lap who was supposed to be his wife in a couple of weeks, was asking weird questions: "do you like threesome?"

***

He found himself in a dream, again. When he looked forward he saw the daylight, but the darkness of the night was following right behind him.

The 'thing' also was at his back. It did not seem in a hurry to catch him. This was like playing cat and mouse. Hayri would be the mouse and the cat was the thing, blowing its fiery breaths on his neck.

He was terrified. He wanted to run, to fly, get away from this thing, but his feet were planted in concrete. He tried to scream, to shout or to roar. But no sound came out from his mouth.

"Courage, courage! This is nothing but a nightmare," he told himself, trying to calm down.

If he could just take a look at back, to see that THING!

His curiosity was stronger than his fear but he could never turn his head, although he had no longer the brace around the neck. He forced himself to move once again and run away but did not succeed.

When he tried to scream again, a horrible sound burst from his mouth. This inhuman scream, was-it really coming out of his own mouth? Anyway the scream woke him up, rescuing him from the nightmare.

Breathless, he stood up from the bed. His whole body was soaked with sweat. It was clear this thing had not abandoned him and it was showing up whenever he missed taking the sleeping pill.

***

It is five o'clock, Paris awakes
It is five o'clock, I am still awake[51]

When he heard this song, he instinctively looked at his watch. It was almost 5am. God knows for how long he had been wandering like a ghost in the streets.

[51] Lyrics of a popular French song.

After futile attempts to sleep, he decided to get up. As it was too late to take his sleeping pill, he decided to stay awake for the rest of the night. He decided to go out, yet he felt very tired.

The music was coming from a café-bar. The waiter who was busy cleaning the entrance, said “bonjour monsieur” to him.

“Do you have fresh coffee?”

“Of course monsieur, please enter. I'll be right with you,” said the waiter.

The boss was behind the bar.

“Hello monsieur,” he said, smiling.

Hayri asked for a black coffee.

“Right away, monsieur,” said the boss.

He sat down at a table where he could see the people in the street. They all looked in hurry. They were almost running toward the subway station and disappearing at the stairs going to the underground.

He watched a blonde woman with high heels. She was also running. She crossed the street to get to the subway. Just before putting her foot on the opposite sidewalk, she nearly lost her balance but recovered quickly and began to run as if nothing happened. She was lucky not to have been a sprain.

The waiter brought him his coffee.

“Would you like to eat something, monsieur?”

“No, thank you.”

The waiter had a Turkish accent. But Hayri had no desire to speak to anyone. Except perhaps to Nadir.

He returned his eyes to the street, he couldn't see that woman in high heels. She had already disappeared.

These people he was observing, they all seemed to have slept well last night, unlike him. They probably had not had a nightmare and they were certainly not followed by the 'thing'.

This 'thing', this is how he kept calling it. It would also been called monster, dragon, spectrum, shadow, etc....

During the nightmares, he was curious to look back in order to see what was following him. But each, time he missed the courage to do that. He blamed the brace around his neck which wasn't even there anymore.

But where was this Turk, the bravest man in the world? He murmured with a bitter smile.

Here! The boss catches him smiling. He is probably going to take him for a crackpot.

***

The first phone call of the day came on his cell as he was climbing the stairs of Sacré-Coeur Cathedral in Montmartre. This was his mother. She had returned home from hospital and was surprised not to find her son at home.

"Are you okay?"

"Yes Mom, I'm fine. I wanted to take a walk for a little fresh air.

Damn! He forgot to put the whiskey bottle back to the cupboard. Hopefully she would not go into his room.

“How is the daughter of Madame Hermine?” he asked.

“She gave birth to a boy. You should see how beautiful the baby is.

“I know,” thought Hayri. “Babies are always beautiful.”

“Madame Hermine gave me the key to her apartment. I came to get some items she needs. We were pressed yesterday and we forgot some important items before going to the hospital.”

“So are going back, immediately?”

“Yes Hayri, goodbye.”

“Goodbye Mom.”

Apparently, the newborn was making her happy.

He set his cell phone in silent mode before putting it back into his pocket. When he finally reached the top of the hill, he was out of breath. He regretted not taking the funicular. Was he getting older?

Paris was giving a clear view despite the gray sky. The sun, having found a hole in the clouds, was sending its rays to the domes of the old basilica. He sat on the last top step, a few yards away from a couple who were kissing.

His BlackBerry vibrated. This must be his mother again. She probably would give him some instructions. He took it from his pocket without haste and pressed the button to answer.

“What is it again, mom?”

After a short silence, a female voice spoke. It was not his mother.

"This is Esther. I hope I'm not disturbing?"

Esther? But does he know someone of that name? Yet his interlocutor had a sweet voice, even sexy. This was probably a mistake.

"We met Saturday evening, at the dinner at the Turkish restaurant," she said.

Ah, yes! This is the German woman. So, Esther was her name?

"Hello Esther. How are you?"

"I'm fine, thank you. So, are we agreed for Thursday night to go to the theater?"

"Yes, yes. You already have the tickets, right?"

"Yes, I do. I think I already told you that while we were at the restaurant."

But of course, she said that. How could he forget?

"Today I'm going to Orleans[52] to continue my research, she said."

"Your research?"

"For my book. Remember" I told you. I will consult the old documents about Joan of Arc, original manuscripts in microfiche."

She told him all that? He remembered vaguely. Oh, yes. She has a PhD. What was her subject?

"Are you going to make a historical research?" he asked, to look interested.

[52] Orleans: A city at about 80 miles at the south of Paris.

“No. I work on the psychology of people. Thousands of people had followed Joan of Arc. She was nothing but a young girl. I will try to understand the reasons for this miraculous event.”

He remembered that she was a psychologist, like Nadir. Were they both interested in him because he had problems? She had seen his brace. Did he told him about his nightmares? He remembered that as usual, he had drunk too much. He could have told her anything.

“When are you going return from Orleans? Tomorrow night?”

“I do not think I'll be able to finish all in one day. And I also have to meet there a professor from Yale.”

“Ah! Academicians,” thought Hayri. Fortunately, he did not have to travel with her, because he might fall into the ‘trap’ and start chatting on unnecessary subjects.

“I think I'll spend the night in a hotel in Orleans and come back after tomorrow. The trip with train is about an hour. On my return to Paris, I have ample time to prepare. Would you like to go to dinner together, before the theater?”

This was an invitation that a gentleman could not refuse.

“Sure,” said Hayri.

“The show starts at eight. I’ll meet you around 6pm. We will have about two hours. I think this is enough time for a dinner.”

“Sure”.

They said goodbye and hung up. As usual, he was letting himself be led by women. This was not a good sign.

Obviously, she was interested in him. Yet, he didn't even try to flirt. He remembered the words of an old friend:

> *"Ah, Germans, once out of their country, all of a sudden they become good friends of Turks."*
>
> *"Why?" had asked Hayri.*
>
> *"Maybe because both nations have kind of same destiny to share."*

The step he was sitting on, began to make him feel the cold at the buttocks. He stood up. What he needed now, was to sit in a comfortable chair of one of the cafés. He had come here to see the Place du Tertre[53].

Finally free from the clouds, the sun was starting to make shadows on the square which was yet empty. In a few hours, there would be hundreds of people here. The weather was still cool. He picked an armchair in a cafe and ordered a chocolate.

His BlackBerry vibrated for the third time. He had made the mistake of not having completely shut it down. Seeing 'Sinan' on the screen, he decided to answer. He could not refuse a call from an old friend.

"Where are you?" asked Sinan Bey

Ah, but this was unbelievable! He was worse than his mother. He wants to know everything.

But Hayri tried to reply politely:

[53] The Place du Tertre: a square near the Sacré-Cœur Cathedral, with its many artists setting up their easels.

“I'm in a café.” Needless to give details, he told himself.

“I have news for you,” Sinan Bey. The investigation is closed.

“But you already said that, didn’t you?”

Sinan Bey laughed.

“Would you ever have forgotten that you had been hospitalized last week?”

“No, but?”

“Good. So are you okay? Your neck, your nightmares?”

“I am in good shape. What are you trying to say?”

The silence on the other end, let him understand that Sinan Bey doubted his sincerity. Maybe he would try another question.

“Did the divers of the police find the object that the man in coma has allegedly thrown to the River Seine?”

Sinan Bey still remained silent for a few seconds, then he answered:

« You're curious, huh? If they had found something important, they would not have closed the case, would they? And I have also been informed that this ‘object’, supposedly thrown into the river, appears only in the testimony of a clochard[54]. One of those old tramps who still continue to live under the bridges. These men are eternal, you know, they are like the monuments of Paris.

Those words were surprising. This is the first time that Hayri was hearing from Sinan Bey something that could be considered positive for the French.

[54] Vagabond of Paris.

“Next week, I am organizing a dinner.”

“In the Pideci, like the last time?” asked Hayri.

“I don’t know yet. Many of the Turkish residents will come. I will also invite a couple of friends who are in visit in Paris. I must look for a larger restaurant.

Communication was cut off before he finished his sentence. Hayri looked at his Blackberry. There was nothing on the screen. The battery was flat. He had forgotten to recharge.

“Ah! Sinan Bey,” thought Hayri. “Always trying to organize the Turks. Wasted effort.”

***

When he saw the bridge, by far, his heart began to beat. Yet, this was not the bridge over which his father was murdered. After all, it was nothing but an accident. One of the many accidents that occur every day in Paris. Why did he return to this place like a ‘guilty’ man who always returns to the scene of the crime? He was not responsible for the accident. He was not even driving. So, why all this excitement?

He walked to the middle of the bridge and looked down towards the Seine. The river was muddy in color and repulsive.

“I need to see that at night, under the lights,” he thought.

On the platform below, there was a kissing couple. A boat full of tourists approached with projectors stronger than the day light.

He began to walk across the bridge and approached the spot where the man had been hit by the car, in which he was a passenger. He tried to locate the exact spot of the accident.

It was not easy. He remembered a car with the alarm sounding and the police asking him questions. Questions that, under the influence of alcohol, he gave weird answers. And finally an ambulance and hospitalization.

He was in front of a hair salon for women. One of hairdressers inside approached the door and asked:

"Looking for someone, monsieur?"

This was a young girl. She had probably taken Hayri for a tourist who was searching for an address.

"I had an accident in the street last week. I was curious...."

The girl had a very big surprise.

"But how come you are standing? The car had hit you very hard."

"Did you see the accident?"

"Oh, yes monsieur."

Hayri had to explain that he was not the one who was hit. He was in the car, but sitting on the back seat.

"Ah, well, she said. And how is the other man?"

The man she called 'other' was still in a coma but Hayri would not give her this detail.

"I think he is still in the hospital," he said.

"Really? Is he going to recover?"

"I hope so," he said, avoiding the curious gaze of the young hairdresser.

An authoritative female voice boomed from inside:

"Annie, are you done?"

This was the boss. The girl moved immediately away from the door. Hayri also withdrew not put the young girl in trouble.

He walked slowly along the sidewalk. After a few steps, something flickering between two cars parked along the street caught his attention. Curious, he went to pick it up. It was a small piece of broken glass, yellow, probably from the signal light of a car.

A satisfied smile covered his face. He wrapped it like a jewel in his handkerchief and put in his pocket.

His stomach has started to cry famine. It was almost noon and he had not eaten since the night before.

***

Fourth session

"The language of every nation reveals its character," said Nadir.

They were both sitting in the comfortable chairs in the quiet corner of a cafe. Nadir had decided to make the fourth session out of the hospital. He explained the stages of therapy: "Usually a kind of resistance develops in the patient towards the fourth or the fifth session. So far, everything went well with you. But I do not want to lose you. So today, we will talk here for a change."

“How can a language reveal the character of a nation?” asked Hayri.

“You're a polyglot, like me. You speak three languages. Let us try to compare the English with the French.”

He stood up. Making exaggerated gestures with his hands, he showed the aisle between the tables and chairs rows.

“You see this passage that goes straight to the exit? Let us assume this is the English language,” he said loudly.

Some curious customers stopped their conversations to watch him. Hayri embarrassed, leaned back in his chair. Nadir, walked to the middle of the café and began to move tables and chairs.

The boss protested:

“But monsieur! What are you doing?”

Nadir gestured with his arm to calm him.

“Don’t worry, monsieur. I'll put everything back to their places. Allow me a few seconds, please. I'm trying to explain something to my friend.”

Heads turned to Hayri who sank further into the armchair. Nadir, like an actor, was spectacular with his turban de maharajah. Tables and chairs moved, the room turned to the backstage of a medieval Indian theater.

“You see,” he said. “Now to go out, you have to find your way through this labyrinth.”

Then he began to arrange the tables and chairs. Hayri rose to help. The owner of the cafe continued to observe. His anger was overcome by his curiosity. He said nothing.

When everything was in place, Nadir returned to his seat. Hayri wanted to leave.

“So, this labyrinth you just saw, was the French language,” said Nadir.

Hayri had a laugh that he regretted immediately. He saw the boss walking towards them.

“Gentlemen! If you do not behave, please go!”

He was right. Hayri left a ten euro note on the table, stood up and walked towards the exit. Nadir followed.

They did not exchange a word on the way back. It was a great relief for Hayri when they finally entered Nadir’s office. He decided not to go out with this man again. Nadir wanted to continue with the conversation that he had begun at the café:

“So what do you think of my idea?”

“What idea?”

“That the French language is like a labyrinth.”

Hayri had the same laugh he had in the café before being driven out by the boss. This man, although strange, had a nice side. Hayri could never make confession to someone else before him. He was more or less sharing his opinion about the complexity of the French language but he wanted to play devil’s advocate, to see his reaction.

“But French is often preferred in international debates. I witnessed that on several occasion. I am a diplomat, remember?”

“But that's exactly what I'm trying to explain, my friend. French is a diplomatic language.”

“So?”

“Think about it Hayri. ‘Diplomatic’; what does it mean?”

“..?”

Nadir had a mischievous smile.

“This means you can say one thing but mean another. For example, you can always say: But your Excellency, you misunderstood. I did not mean this, but that.”

“I think you can make this kind demagoguery in more or less all languages,” said Hayri.

“But none could achieve the quality that you can find in the French language,” said Nadir, with a large smile.

Was it a compliment or a criticism? It was difficult to know. But this wasn’t Hayri’s concern anyway. He was feeling tired. This was enough for today. So he asked nicely if they could continue the next day.

“No problem,” said Nadir.

Just before leaving, Hayri had the idea to tell him what he did today.

“I was at the place of the accident.”

Nadir could not hide his surprise.

“Really? I'd like to hear about that. Can you stay for a few minutes and tell me the details of your visit to this place, and especially the reason?”

“The reason? I honestly do not know. But the ‘guilty’ returns always to the scene of the crime, they say.”

Nadir's surprise increased.

“Do you think you're responsible for the accident?”

“Technically not. But if I had refused to be driven home with the car of Madam Consul, if I had taken a taxi or the subway, the driver would probably have chosen another path and the accident wouldn’t happen.”

“Ah, I see. So, you believe in fate.”

Before answering him, Hayri felt the need to think a little. The man in front of him, with his turban, was probably believing even in reincarnation. But Hayri, himself, he was nothing but an agnostic about spiritual believes. Not knowing what to say, he gave him a big smile. He took out of his pocket the piece he had packed in his handkerchief.

“And there, I found this.”

Nadir put his glasses and leaned to see.

“You found it on the site of the accident?”

“Yes. It must be a broken piece of signal light of a car. We had hit one of the cars parked along the curb. I do not know if this piece belongs to our car or to another.”

“So you have to continue with your personal investigation,” said Nadir.

Hayri gave a puzzled look. This man did not seem to be joking. He was serious.

***

“This is ridiculous!” he whispered. But there he was again, the place where the accident had happened. The scene of crime that the ‘criminal’ always return.

It was almost nine o’clock in the evening. Worthy of its name, the ‘city of lights’ was shining everywhere. Leaning on the railing of the bridge, he watched the Seine. A black barge, in contrast with the bright decor, was passing below slowly. In the distance, he could see the Eiffel Tower, sparkling.

Everything was beautiful, too beautiful. The words of an old friend came to his mind: “Paris is like a woman wearing too much makeup. If you remove the makeup, below you will find nothing but a whore.”

Whenever he remembered that comment, he smiled. Despite everything, Hayri loved this ‘whore’.

He was feeling like in a nice dream. His eyes wandering everywhere, focused finally to an approaching tourist boat. It was projecting its bright lights on the banks of the river.

He heard someone singing:

How would you like to be
Down by the Seine with me

He leaned over to see if came from another ship passing under. Tourists sitting at round tables were having dinner and taking landscape photos with flash without stopping.

“None of the photos will be good,” he said, remembering what he had learned about photography course during his college years.

The pleasant song continued to caress his ears.

Oh what I'd give for a moment or two
Under the bridges of Paris with you

This tenor voice could not come from the tourist boat that was already disappearing under the bridge. Intrigued, his eyes searched the banks of the Seine. Without the projectors of the boat, everything was plunged back to the dark.

Firsts he saw nothing. When his eyes were adjusted, he saw a shadow. A man walking slowly on the platform of the left bank. He was walking with a slight limp. No doubt, this was the singer.

Darling I'd hold you tight
Far from the eyes of night.

“This man is probably happier than me,” thought Hayri. “He has a beautiful voice and is singing like an opera singer.”

The vagabonds go there at night
To sleep all their troubles away,
But when the moon is shining bright
My heart wants to sing it this way.

The man approached a couple who were kissing on the dock. Hayri heard him saying:

“Do you have some wine, lady and gentleman?”

The couple was too busy to listen. With no response, the vagabond continued to walk. In a few moments, he would be too far, swallowed by the night.

The devil who had watched the scene from the beginning, touched Hayri's shoulder with his invisible hand and whispered him in the ear:

"Go and talk to him!"

Why the best ideas come always from the devil?

He had noticed a grocery store on his way here. He walked back hoping to find it still open. He was lucky, the store was open despite the late hour. An old lady behind the counter asked:

"Good evening monsieur. What do you want?"

"I would like to buy a bottle of wine, please."

She showed a bottle.

"I recommend this."

"How much?"

"Forty euros."

"Oh no, said Hayri. I just want a bottle that costs only a few euros."

"Ah!" she said, disappointed. "You want an ordinary wine."

That was the word to say: ordinary, and the price was qualifying it.

She did not fail to ask the question that seemed necessary for customers purchasing the 'ordinary' wine:

"Do you want me to open the bottle, monsieur?"

"Oh, yes, please," said Hayri, smiling.

When he came to the bridge, the vagabond was invisible.

He walked down the stairs. Same couple was still there, kissing. A shadow was walking about thirty yards away. Hayri slowed down his steps not to frighten him.

The man hearing footsteps stopped and turned his head back to look. Seeing Hayri, he made an exaggerated gesture to greet him.

"Ah! My lord, the king! What an honor!"

Not only was he drunk, but he was also crazy. His gaze turned immediately to the package Hayri was holding in his hand. Although the bottle was packed, it was not difficult for a drunkard -an expert in the field- to guess what it could be.

"What your majesty wishes tonight from his humble servant?" he asked.

The projectors of another boat, smaller this time, flooded the stage with light. Hayri could accurately distinguish the face of the vagabond. Contrary to what he had originally imagined, he did not seem too old. He had a cheerful face and seemed harmless.

"Do you have wine, young man?"

Ah! He was down-graded from his 'majesty' to the young man. But Hayri found his new title even more flattering. After all, who wouldn't want to be young?

"Yes, I have a bottle of wine. Would you like to share with me?"

Hayri could not see the expression on his face, but he was sure the man was smiling. He unwrapped the bottle and handed it to him.

The man, after taking a big gulp,

"I am a tenor, you know?" he said.

"I heard you singing. You have a beautiful voice."

"I sang in opera when I was young."

"Really?

"You don't believe me?"

"Of course I believe you," said Hayri.

"You must say "*tu*[55]", young man!" he said, with an authoritative voice.

"Ah, French!" thought Hayri. "Always proud to have second person singular in their language. One thing the English don't have."

The man began to sing an aria. He sang well enough. He was perhaps a real opera tenor. Hayri waited for him to finish his song.

"Are you retired now? You sing no more at the Opera?"

"They fired me ten years ago. And now I sing under the bridges, by the Seine."

"Are you homeless?"

"I am known in my neighborhood. I have some concierge-friends who let me sleep in the cellars of their buildings, at cold winter nights."

---

[55] Tu (thou): Second person singular in French. You.

"The life of this man must be very difficult, especially if he was a real opera tenor once," thought Hayri.

"Why did they let you go?"

"They are the Republicans[56]! They destroy everything," said the man.

"I see," replied Hayri.

He was curious to know where this conversation would go. Did he start drinking before or after he lost his position at the opera?

The man began to criticize the society. He spoke quickly and Hayri could not understand all the words he said. But he could still understand some of them: bastards, unjust, Republicans, fraudsters, goons…

"The Republicans, they are all bastards! Don't agree young man?" he asked finally.

Tonight, Hayri had no reason to contradict him. And he liked to be called 'young' man.

"But of course monsieur," he replied.

The man handed him the bottle which was already empty and shouted:

"So, long live the king!"

The kissing-couple near the stairs heard that and turned their heads to look.

"Ah! He is a royalist, the old man," the said girl with a laughter.

Hayri bit his lip to hide a smile.

Suddenly he remembered his reason for being here.

[56] Referring to the war between the Royalists and the Republicans during the French Revolution.

"Do you often wander on the docks during the day, monsieur?"

He forgot to address him in "*tu*" but the man did not notice the error.

"Yes. I spend almost all my days and nights here. When the bedtime comes, I go to find one of my concierge friends."

"Do you know that last week there was an accident up in the street?"

He pointed with his hand the scene of the accident.

"I heard the crash and I went upstairs to see. A man was hit. He has been hospitalized."

Hayri saw no reason not to tell him everything.

"I was in the car but it wasn't me who was driving."

Another boat with lights was passing. The man's face became serious. He came to watch Hayri closely.

"I remember now," he said. "I saw you. They put a brace around your neck. Are you okay now? Nothing serious?"

"Nothing serious," replied Hayri, surprised by the memory of the man.

He revised the words in his brain before asking the right question to the man.

"I heard that this man, before being hit by the car, threw something into the Seine. It is also said that the police divers have made a search in the river but found nothing."

The man's face became even more serious.

"Of course," he said. "They can't find something that is not there."

"What do you mean?"

“Just before the accident, I saw him throwing a bag over the bridge. But the bag did not fall into the water.”

“How come?” asked Hayri, surprised.

The man smiled for the first time.

“A barge was passing. The bag fell into the barge.

“Oh!”

“It has never been in the water. How do you want the divers to find it? God knows where it is now.”

This was explaining everything. There was one last question left:

“But why didn’t you say that to the police?”

“I do not speak with Republicans, young man! You're a royalist, right?”

“But of course,” said Hayri smiling.

“You see now why I am telling you everything?”

“I see.”

“So, long live the king!”

“Long live the king!”

***

Midnight was past when Hayri finally returned to his apartment. In the living room, he found his mother asleep in a chair. She was probably very worried about the sudden disappearance of his son. He had the wake her up gently and give some ‘logical’ explanations.

He did not fail to put his BlackBerry to charge before going to bed. He did not fail to take a sleeping pill either. Once in bed, he began to think what the vagabond had told him tonight.

This man who was still in a coma, had thus really threw something into the Seine, just before he was hit by the car.

And now Hayri was a royalist.

"Long live the king!" he said, stifling a laugh into the blanket, not to wake up his mother.

He was a royalist, with no king.

VII

The roots of education are bitter
but the fruits are sweet.
Aristotle

The Labyrinth of Francophiles

Hayri was shaving in the bathroom when heard a strange noise, like a baby playing with a rattle.

“Mom! What is this?” he asked loud for her to hear.

“It's your phone,” she said from the kitchen.

She was right. The ringing was coming from the bedroom. How did he forget that he has a BlackBerry?

“I need to change this annoying ring tone,” he said, walking out of the bathroom with his face covered with foam. The ring stopped before he could reach the phone.

The phone in the living room took over. He ran and picked it up. A female voice froze him.

“Hayri Bey?”

Oops! It was Madam Consul.

“Ah! Hello Madam Consul. How are you?”

“I'm fine. But I was worried about you. Yesterday, despite my best efforts, I couldn’t reach you. You did not answer neither to this phone, nor your cell. I even thought to send someone home, to see if all was well. Then I had the idea to call Sinan Bey. He called the hospital to talk to your doctor who gave him the phone of another doctor. A psychologist. What was his name...?”

“Udayasekaran?”

“Yes, it is. Mr. Udayasekaran. Why do you consult a psychologist?”

Damn! She was aware of the therapy. She could now take him for a psychopath.

It was all his fault anyway. He acted as if he was on vacation. What was expected of him after the accident, was sitting at home and rest. Certainly not wandering in the streets.

He tried to find an excuse:

“Yesterday, I felt well. I was bored at home I went for a walk around a bit before going to see the psychologist. The doctor who treated my neck, suggested me to see psychologist if there was a psychological trauma caused by the accident. All is well. Nothing to worry about. My mother and I, we were both out yesterday. She was...”

"I am happy to know that you are well," said the consul, sharply cutting his speech.

One could feel a slight irony in her voice.

"Thank you Madam Consul. Do you want me to come to the office today?"

"No, no. Do not come back until the end of your leave. Your return is scheduled for next Monday, isn't it?"

"Yes, Madam Consul."

"Then I'll see on Monday. And do not forget that the following Wednesday morning we will all be present at the Embassy for the first day of Eid al-Adha[57]. Good bye."

"Yes, Madam Consul," said again Hayri.

But the caller does not hear his last words, she had already hung up.

Oops! This was not good. Apparently, she was a little angry. He had completely forgotten that he had a job. He had been acting irresponsibly.

***

Fifth session

"Did you sleep well, last night?" asked Nadir.

"Very well, but I'm a little dizzy, still under the influence of pill," said Hayri.

Should he tell him about the vagabond he met under the bridge?

[57] Festival of the Sacrifice of Muslims.

“So today, what are you going to tell me? In the last session, you told me about your return to Turkey, after the murder of your father?”

‘The murder of your father.’ Those words made him shudder. He remained silent for a few moments.

“When do you think I will be cured?” he asked.

“Are you tired of the sessions?”

“Tired? No, but I must return to my normal life as soon as possible and start working.”

“I think you're ready to return to work. As for the sessions, I prefer that you keep coming. You're right in the middle of the program.”

“Program?”

Nadir had an indulgent look.

“Yes, the ‘program’. So far, we are doing well. You're on the right track. But if you quit now, your nightmares will come back and it will be even harder for me to heal you.”

Then smiling, he added:

“Heal. I believe this is the word that suits you, better than ‘cure’.”

“I understand that if we stop now it will be harder later. But why?” Hayri asked.

“I think I already told you. If you interrupt the sessions, you'll give your subconscious the opportunity to develop a defense system. This will make all the future efforts ineffective for treatment. With my method, you have one chance to succeed. I advise you to continue without stopping. We are close to success. A little patience, this is all what is needed!"

Doctor looked upset. He did not even try to hide his emotions. Hayri felt the need to say something to calm him:

"Mr. Udayasekaran. I trust you and I promise to continue the sessions."

"Thank you," replied the doctor, relieved.

"Next week, Wednesday is the first day of a religious holiday. I am expected to the Embassy for a ceremony."

"It is for Eid al-Adha, isn't it? The festival where Muslims slaughter animals?" said Nadir.

Hayri - although he was not religious - felt offended.

"You are Buddhist, aren't you?"

"I do not practice it, but I am still a vegetarian."

They exchanged a smile.

"I'm agnostic," said Hayri. "But if necessary, I can prove that I am a Muslim."

"How?"

Hayri took a card out from his pocket and showed him.

"This is my National Identity Card. Look at the part 'religion'. What do you see?"

Nadir took his glasses and leaned close to read the word 'Islam'.

"You see?" said Hayri. "This is the official proof. My religion is well Islam."

"Is it mandatory in your country, to put this information in identity cards?"

"Not really," said Hayri. "I have actually the right to replace it with another religion or deleted it completely. But what is curious, this information was registered at my birth!"

"When you were born?"

"Exactly! When I was a newborn!"

There has been a silence. Then Nadir spoke:

"I will not comment on it. But now, you're going to tell me the story of your return to Turkey, right? Would you please start?"

Hayri obeyed and began to speak:

"The shock was so great for me that I wasn't even able to cry. I would never have thought that my father could die. My mother, who lost her beloved husband, she of course cried. She was a widow now. For women, it is okay to cry, right? Especially for her who has never missed any 'occasion' for crying. She would find any excuse to have eyes flooded with tears. I even remember her crying, when I was a child, because I refused to eat a tomato."

"A tomato?"

"Ah! I must explain you something. Tomato has a very important position in Turkish culture. For example, you should never tell a Turk that you do not like tomatoes. He might feel offended and will immediately begin to give you a speech on the benefits of this wonder of nature. But I always hated that stuff!"

They were silent for a few moments. Nadir was listening carefully, however they were not here to talk about tomatoes, were they?

"But I must also admit that since the death of my father, my mother stopped crying for stupid things."

There was a silence gain for couple of seconds...

"Before our return to Turkey, my mother wrote a letter to her friends. She was looking for a job. She needed something to keep her busy. A job was arranged for her in Ankara. She was supposed to start in September. I wanted to be with my mother, but she insisted I register at the School of Frères[58] in Istanbul."

"Why?" Nadir asked, finally breaking his silence.

"To avoid that I forget the French. This would also be the desire of my father. Francophonie was a family tradition. So I obeyed."

Hayri was often interrupting his own narration. The words should be chosen carefully. He was aware of one thing. The real reason of his presence here was not to tell his life story. Due to cultural differences, this famous psychologist, would not understand even half of the things he was hearing.

On the other hand, Hayri was reviewing of his own life. He was speaking to himself and sometimes forgetting that he was in the presence of Nadir.

"Early one morning, a limo from the Embassy took us quietly to another city. The idea was to avoid reporters who were watching us day and night.

[58] Originally Catholic school giving secular education in French language.

And we took the plane from there. My father's coffin was placed in another plane in Paris."

"When we arrived in Ankara, a crowd was waiting at the airport."

He paused for a moment and remained pensive. Everything was like a movie, a scary one.

"We spent two weeks in a hotel. It was painful. Journalists were waiting in the street to see us. They wanted to talk with the widow and the orphan."

"According to plan, I would be an intern in School of Frères in Istanbul. As for my mother, she rented an apartment in Ankara, in the center of the city to be close to the Department where she would start working.

"When everything was ready, we went to Istanbul to spend a few weeks with my aunt, before the school starts. Her house was in Erenköy. This is a suburb of the city was known with its large houses and large gardens. To go to school, I would take the train and the passenger boat. But since I was going to be boarded at the school, I would need to make this trip on weekends only.

Nadir interrupted:

"Tell me about the school. What did you study?"

"This is a private French school, founded in the seventeenth century by the Jesuits and I think they started to welcome first Muslim students in late nineteenth century."

Nadir was surprised again.

"Why on earth a Muslim would study in a Christian school?"

“I think this was the fashion in the Ottoman Empire in late nineteenth century, and I think this fashion still goes on,” said Hayri, attempting a smile.

Nadir smiled too. After all, he was also coming from a country where English was the official language. So he would understand.

Hayri continued:

“My mother left me at school in Istanbul and returned to Ankara.”

“You were a little boy. Did you feel alone?”

“Alone? I would rather say abandoned.”

“Did the students wear uniforms?”

Why does he want to know so much detail?

“No, but we were all dressed in jacket and tie.”

The image of the first day was before his eyes. All students and teachers were present in the large courtyard. They first sang the National Anthem. After a long speech by the headmaster, the teachers had taken them into classes.

“During the first week there was no study after class. We were having some relaxed time in the courtyard then we were going to the dorms. The lights were extinguishing at 9pm sharp. With the lights out, I was hiding under the blanket. Trying to cry, unsuccessfully. I had totally lost my ability to cry.”

“Did you get along well with your friends?”

“Yes, but I was the ‘nouveau[59]’. Majority of students knew each other, already. They had started the school all together four years ago. The school normally lasts eight years. For my part, I was directly starting as the eighth grader; the equivalent of the third grader[60] in France. So I was forced to undergo my *bizutage*[61]."

Nadir's smile made him understand that he knew the meaning of the word.

Another memory made him smile. His classmates had taken him to the water, which meant 'soak the guy'. The new guys were simply forced to take a shower with his clothes on. Soaked to the bone, he had to sit in math class for forty five minutes.

Nadir noticed that smile on his face but did not ask the reason. Obviously, Hayri was remembering many more things but wasn't telling everything.

"A few weeks later, I had already made me a social environment. The majority of students in my class were, as we sometimes say, 'non-Muslims'. This odd title has always struck me as. This is one way of denying someone who is different from yourself. It always reminds me of Venn diagrams, in mathematics."

"Venn diagrams?"

Hayri chuckled.

"May I use your computer? It will be easier for me to show on the screen rather than trying to explain it with words."

"Help yourself," said Nadir, with a gesture of invitation.

Hayri got up to sit on the chair in front of the PC, checked first he was well connected to the Internet and typed the words 'Venn diagrams' to initiate a

[59] Nouveau (Fr.): The new guy.
[60] In French school system, classes are numbered in reverse order: from eleven towards one.
[61] Bizutage (Fr.): Hazing, bullying.

search. Google returned him a dozen answers in English. He chose one. Several colored circles began to appear on the screen.

“Suppose this one represents Muslims”, he said, pointing to one of the circles.

Nadir was looking over his shoulder.

“I see where you're going,” he said. “All those who remain outside that circle represent the non-Muslims, right?”

“Exactly.”

“Hayri, would you be a symbolist by any chance?” asked Nadir, with a funny look.

Symbolism. Hayri’s French teacher had explained the meaning of this word, in class. And at the university, he had taken the course of Symbolic Logic from an Indian professor, though he did not consider himself a symbolist.

“No,” he said. “I don’t think so. And I do not like the representation of living creatures by geometric figures.”

“What about the example you just gave me?”

“This is my approach to the problem. Because I believe that the word non-Muslim is nothing but a form of discrimination! I was just trying to be sarcastic.”

They stared each other silently. One could see in their eyes that these two men understood each other.

Nadir walked towards the window and spoke murmuring. Hayri had to pay attention to hear him.

“For example, the color of the skin is an individual characteristic and often regarded as an ethnic marker. It can also be represented with Venn diagrams.”

Then he turned with a bitter smile on his lips:

“Don’t you think so?”

Was it possible that Hayri offended him without knowing?

Nadir's smile suddenly changed into a laugh:

“But enough with jokes. Tell me more about your school adventures.”

“Among students, there were Jews, Armenians, Greeks, Italians and even some French. We Turks, we were only the third of the population.”

“You, the Turks?”

“Yes, we the Turks.”

“And the others? Were they of different nationalities?

Hayri realized immediately his mistake and corrected:

“What I meant -speaking of Venn diagrams- we were all in the same circle. We were all Turks. But apart from this common circle, we also had our small circles for each religion.

“I see,” said Nadir.

Hayri remembered a joke from one of his Jewish friends: “Muslim and Jewish men have a common circle,” he had said. When he had explained the reason, Hayri had laughed. It was during math class and the angry teacher had put them outside the door. They had to report to the superintendent before being readmitted to class.

This memory made him smile. Nadir noticed that smile and asked for the reason. Hayri had to tell him the story.

“And what is it that common thing that puts Jews and Muslims in the same circle?”

Hayri had to explain:

“They are both circumcised. Others are not.”

Nadir smiled too.

“I can see that you have learned well, the Venn diagrams.”

Obviously, what Hayri had just told, had amused him.

“But do you see, Hayri?” said Nadir. “You have been lucky. It was this school that placed all of you in a single circle, a large circle of different cultures.”

“Yes, I do.”

“It was a chance for you. A chance that in this world, many other people never had.”

“Of course.”

“So, why do you hate the French, Hayri?”

“But what makes you think I hate the French?”

“That's the impression I had, ever since I've known you.”

Ah, psychologists! They think they are capable to infiltrate like spies into our brain.

"You are mistaken. I do not hate the French. Why would I hate them? I'm just not a Francophile, that's all."

Nadir changed the subject.

"Among your memories of high school, do you have other interesting things to tell me?"

"Nothing in particular. We were just kids. Like most of the kids, happy and insouciant."

"No special friends?"

"What do you mean?"

"Someone special, someone you could tell your secrets, share your ideas?"

For a couple of seconds, Hayri thought about it. There was no one special. Or rather, everybody was special, in a way. Between friends, nobody stood out more than others.

But he had forgotten to tell him about Rashad. Rashad he had known during his years in Diyarbakir, in eastern Turkey. Surprisingly, they had met in this French school.

"Do you believe in telepathy?" he asked to Nadir.

"You are asking me if I believe in telepathy?" said Nadir without hiding his surprise. "But why?"

“I had already talked about Rashad. I was very surprised to find him back. He had managed to finish the primary school in Diyarbakir, and he had come to Istanbul to continue his secondary education.”

“Here you meet again.”

“He had changed a little. Not only physically. He was believing that there was a telepathic connection between two of us.”

“Funny. But you do not believe in telepathy, do you?”

“To be honest, I don’t know.”

“What do you mean, you don’t know?”

Hayri didn’t want the doctor takes him for lunatic.

“Rashad believed he was able to read my mind and was capable of sending me messages whenever he wanted.”

“Could he?” asked Nadir.

“Do ‘you’ believe in telepathy, doctor?”

“But of course!”

“There you got me. Actually something weird happened during a physics exam. One particular formula, although I had reviewed several times before the exam, was hard for me to remember. I looked around but all my class mates were busy, heads down on their exam booklets. Obviously nobody was eager to go into the risk of helping another, with the fear of being caught by the teacher. Rashad was sitting in the front row. He turned his head to look at me. He smiled. And all of sudden, I had the formula in the head!”

He gazed Nadir to see his reaction. The doctor seemed more serious than ever.

"And after the exam, I was very surprised when Rashad approached me and asked if I had received the message he sent."

"Did you get good grades, both of you?"

"Yes. And guess what, in the classroom we were the only ones to solve this problem."

Nadir smiled again: "And you still don't believe in telepathy?"

"I still don't know," said Hayri. "Could that be just a coincidence? Do you think that the science…"

His speech was interrupted by a hand gesture of Nadir.

"The science, my friend, is often shy to face things it can't explain. What you just told me, is one of things that happen every day to many people. But science, in such cases, prefer to remain silent. However, it is well known that some scientists do secrete researches on telepathy."

Hayri unwilling to engage in a discussion, went on to tell his story.

"The following days, Rashad has often said he could read my thoughts. There has been case I almost believed. But it was only in one direction. I could not read his mind."

"So, you do think he was able to send to you, whenever he wanted?"

"I do not know. I had no way of knowing if they were my own thoughts or messages from him."

"This could be very interesting case of search," said Nadir.

“Yes. But he also said he could not do that every time. He was only successful when I was ready. Whatever ‘ready’ means. We did some trials in the school yard, holding a few dozen meters distant. Sometimes he managed to guess the number I wrote on a paper.”

“What an amusing game,” said Nadir. “What did your friends say about this magical event?”

“Others were making fun of us. As Rashad failed to guess the numbers sometimes, his success could only be coincidence.”

Nadir rose from his chair, walked to the window again. It was already dark outside.

“And then, what happened between you and him?”

“What do you mean?” asked Hayri with a nervous voice.

Nadir, turning his back to the window, looked straight into his eyes.

“I feel that something has happened between you two. Did you quarrel?”

This man! Was he by any chance capable of reading minds, too?

Hayri did not want to talk about his bad memory with Rashad. But he had to. It was too late to step back.

“I was a little worried with his ‘magical’ skill. Was my brain betraying me and revealing him my secret thoughts? What if he really knew everything? I wanted to do something he could not foresee: a kind of revenge.”

He paused for a moment to think. Would he tell the rest of the story?

“One morning, I went to the showers. I opened the curtain of a cabin without checking if there was already someone inside. I saw him naked in the shower. My surprise was great when I noticed he was not circumcised! I talked about this to others. This was a serious mistake. A kind of war began in philosophy class. Muslim students, finding allies among the Jews, started to mock with 'uncircumcised' Christians. Paper balls were flying back and forth. The poor teacher, too old to maintain the discipline in class, was crying of anger and trying to reestablish the order, in vain."

Hayri cast a guilty glance at Nadir before continuing.

"Rashad stopped talking to me for about a month. Then one day, he told me he would return to his country[62]. He said his sister was going back too. I was surprised to learn he had a sister in Istanbul. He had never told me before. Apparently she was a student in the French School of Sisters[63]."

"Before his departure, he told me something else: We will meet again!

[62] The word "country" is sometimes used as "my town" in Turkish. This also gives the ambiguous meaning that they consider their own town as a different country.

[63] Catholic school administered by nuns, open also to Muslim female students.

VIII

A weak revenge attracts
a second crime!

Jean Racine, Esther

Esther

Ever since he started to visit Nadir, Hayri could not help seeing all his life flashing before his eyes. This was going on even when he was alone.

After high school, refusing a scholarship of the State, he had chosen a university in Ankara for his studies. His mother tried to persuade him not to turn down that the scholarship which would give him the opportunity to go to a university in France but he did not want to take it. He had neither the desire nor the courage to set foot on French soil, yet.

Of course, there was another reason for him to choose a university in Ankara. The reason was Aysel, the beautiful girl he had met in Bodrum[64] during his summer vacation. She lived in Ankara.

The same year, his mother had decided to retire and move to Istanbul to live with her sister. This wasn't good news because Hayri would have to stay at a residence in the university campus in Ankara. But he would do anything to be near Aysel. The girl he loved so much.

The ringing of the BlackBerry interrupted his thoughts. He answered without looking at the display.

"Hello Hayri. This is Esther."

Ah, this was the German woman. It was nice that she was repeating her name. Although it was always on the tip of his tongue, he did not recall when needed. He also needed to correct his way of referring to her as German lady rather than 'woman', to be polite within himself.

She told she was back from Orleans and wanted to invite him to dinner before the show. They agreed to an appointment at six o'clock, in a restaurant in the 9th[65]. They would have just enough time to eat before the show which would start at 8pm. Hayri noted the address and name of the restaurant on a paper. Then he took the book of Racine from his pocket to put the paper between pages.

He realized that the German lady had the same name as the play they were going to see tonight. Why did she invite him to a play that had the same name of hers?

[64] A favorite vacation place at the south shore of Turkey

[65] One of the administrational divisions of the Paris city, numbered from 1th to 20th.

Putting the book back in his pocket, he smiled. For years, this was the first time that a woman was inviting him to dinner. Did she want to flirt with him?

"But of course!" He murmured with a sly smile. "What else could it be?"

Passersby rushed him quizzical looks.

"Is she beautiful?" he asked himself. It was hard to say. But without doubt, she was *en plein forme*[66]. He had put his hand over his mouth to stifle a second laugh.

Now he was hungry. McDonald's was to the other side of the street but decided to keep his appetite for dinner, he would pass the 'American icon' this time. His feet led him to Edmond Rostand Square again. He must be really loving this area. He walked to the Luxembourg Gardens. Why was he returning here so often?

Arriving at the Great Pond, he began to watch the boys playing with their small sailboats.

Aysel, who had been the only woman he truly loved, came back to his mind. Desolation came over him. Was he still loving her? Yet this woman, who had been his wife, had been unfaithful. And then she was killed in a car accident, with her lover on the driver seat.

First his father, then his wife and then his daughter had died. All were gone, leaving him alone in the world that was becoming increasingly unbearable.

And why was he returned to Paris, after so many years? What was he looking for? His childhood memories?

---

[66] French expression, also used for women slightly over weighted.

The ringing of the BlackBerry pulled him from reveries. He wanted to throw it in the pond. But in the presence of playing children, it would be very inappropriate.

The display showed the number of Sinan Bey. Without bothering to say "hello", he asked Hayri:

"Where are you?

What? Who does this guy think he is? His mother?

"Why?" he asked, trying to make him understand that he was angry.

"I have to talk to you!"

"Why?"

"Where are you?"

"In the Luxembourg Gardens."

"Do not move. I'll get you shortly," he said before hanging up.

Hayri had not even had time to tell him he was standing near the Pond. But he did not care if this 'James Bond' would be able to find him or not. Despite his indifference, he was curious to know what his friend had to say.

His thoughts had evaporated. All of a sudden he was pulled back from the dream to the real world.

A dozen of toy boats were sailing in the pool. Kids were running around with laughter. His eyes met the eyes of the old man who was renting the boats.

"Why not" he told himself and began to walk towards him.

Before reaching the boat guy, someone caught him by the arm. Surprised, he looked into the face of the man who was forcing him to stop. He was even more surprised when the man spoke to him in Turkish:

"Abi! Sinan Bey görüşecek senle, on adım geriden and takip et[67]."

Hayri froze for a moment. Puzzled, he looked behind the man walking towards the exit of the Garden. He had to decide what to do immediately because the man was walking quickly and in a few seconds, he would be lost in the crowd.

After some hesitation he decided to follow the man. It was like the game Cops and Robbers. His guide was walking fast. He was not even turning his head back to check if Hayri was well following him. He went through the doors to the Place Edmond Rostand, crossed the street and began to walk down the Boulevard Saint Michel. After working about hundred meters he stopped and threw a glance back. Then he entered a building. Hayri approached. He read the sign attached to the door:

BOSPHORUS - Internet Café
2st floor.

A bell rang when he pushed the door. On the wall, a small panel-arrow marked Internet Café was indicating a narrow staircase barely visible in the dark. He could hear people talking and laughing; In Turkish naturally.

He hesitated. Would he climb the stairs and see what is up? Or give up playing one of the characters from the novels of John le Carré, turn his back and go back to the street, to the fresh air.

[67] Brother! Sinan Bey wants to talk to you. Follow me ten yards behind.

“Curiosity killed the cat,” he whispered and attacked the stairs. After all, there might be a chance to enjoy a Turkish coffee.

The stairs opened into a large room. There were computers and people. The air was full of smoke and bad smell of cigarette. The man he had followed had disappeared. A young boy, about fifteen years, approached him:

“Buyur abi![68].”

Everything was reminder of a typical coffee house at the outskirts of Ankara or Istanbul.

He heard someone calling the boy behind the counter. The boy gestured with his hand and invited Hayri to follow. Hayri obeyed. They went into a small room behind the counter. There were several stoves on which lined the djezves[69].

The boy opened a small iron gate leading to the outside, to on an iron staircase that would take him down to a small courtyard. Everything smelt damp. He had to be careful not to fall down the slippery steps.

They crossed the court to enter another building. After passing through the dimly lit corridors, they came to a small door. The boy said:

“Abi, go out. You'll see a gray Renault.”

Having said this, the boy turned back and disappeared into the dark corridors. The heart of Hayri began to beat very strong but it was too late to give up. He opened the door.

---

[68] Welcome brother!

[69] Special pots to make Turkish coffee.

The sun blinded him for a moment. When his eyes adjusted to the light, he found a small lane between two buildings, barely wide enough to allow pedestrians to walk. Overflowed garbage bins were all around. Both ends of the lane were opening to streets.

The sound of a car horn coming from left, ended his brief hesitation. A gray Renault was waiting at the end of the lane. He walked toward the car. The back door was open. And of course Sinan Bey was at the driver's seat.

Hayri, out of patience, shouted:

"Sinan Bey! Why this comedy?"

Sinan Bey waved him to be silent.

"Lie down on the bench and cover yourself!"

A blanket lay on the bench. Refusing to obey, he almost growled at him. But Sinan Bey smiled and started the car.:

"Please, do what I am telling you to do. I'll explain in a moment."

Hayri decided to obey. He did not know whether to laugh or be scared. He decided to be patient.

The car drove for about twenty minutes, then stopped. Hayri curious, took blanket off to look outside. They were in an underground car park and the car was parked between others.

"Where are we?" he asked.

"In the parking lot of your hospital," said Sinan Bey.

"My hospital? And why are we here?"

"Soon, it will the time for your appointment with your fakir, right? So I thought this would suit you."

Hayri looked dazed. Then spoke, trying to control his anger:

"Sinan Bey! I do not know what kind of game you want to play. But please be aware that it does not amuse me at all."

"You are being followed, mon cher."

"Followed? By whom?"

Sinan Bey looked him straight in the eye.

We do not know yet but we are sure that you are."

Then he leaned over to open the glove box and pulled out a large envelope and handed it to Hayri.

"Look at these photos!"

Hayri opened the envelope. There were two pictures in black and white. He immediately recognized himself in the first. The shot was taken when he was watching the window of a shop. It should somewhere near the Place de l'Opera or in the Champs Elysées. Beside him, a little backwards, there was somebody else who was looking at the same window.

The second one was taken at night, in a small street not too well lit. There were two men, one behind the other, separated by a dozen yards.

The astonished gaze of Hayri made Sinan Bey smile.

"Is it you in these pictures?" he asked

"I think, yes," answered Hayri. "And the man who follows me, who is he?"

“I told you, we do not know yet. And we do not care of the identity of these men. They are only programmed robots.”

“Oh! They are more than one?”

Sinan Bey smiled again.

“Mon cher, there are several ways of following a man. First of all, the guy should not notice that he is followed. It's a team work. Followers are changed every five or ten minutes, so that you do not notice anything. If you look at the pictures, you'll see it's not the same man.

Hayri looked at the photos again:

“But I can’t see their faces.”

“I have pictures better than these but as I told you, we do not care of their faces or identities. They are just like robots taking orders from…”

“From the robot operators?”

Sinan Bey nodded.

“Probably these men do not even know who you are and why they are following you.”

Hayri paused a moment to think clearly. Then asked:

“Maybe the police are following me?”

“I don’t think so. The French police seem to have no more interest in you. This is more like a private matter.”

Suddenly, an expression of regret crossed his face, as if he had said too much. But continued to talk:

"I mean, this is more like a 'professional' business."

All this was all too much for Hayri. Way too much. His heart began to beat wildly.

"I do not understand. But why? What's going on? You scare me. Maybe I need to return back to Turkey?"

Sinan Bey waved his hand to calm him.

"Do not panic. Foreign diplomats are often followed. That's what we do sometimes, too. I do not think there is a danger for you. You can continue your life normally. But pay attention to the places you frequent."

Hayri jumped on that word.

"Sinan Bey! Who took these pictures?"

"Some of the agents of my team, of course."

"And why your 007 would follow me and take my photos in the streets of Paris, please?" he said, not hiding his anger.

"This is my job, mon cher. I am responsible for all kinds of security of the Turkish delegation in Paris."

"I'm not a senior diplomat! What is the reason for all this nonsense?"

Sinan Bey smirked.

"You might be more important than you think, mon cher."

There has been a silence for a couple of seconds. Then Sinan Bey continued with a calm voice:

"As I told you, I do not think there is a danger for you. However, pay attention to the places you go."

"What do you mean? I am a free man. I have the right to go wherever I want!"

Sinan Bey replied with calm but serious voice:

"A good Turkish diplomat, mon cher, do not go to porn movies."

***

It was almost 3pm and at this hour, the hospital's cafeteria was quiet. Ten minutes had passed since Sinan Bey had left.

Hayri took a coffee. He put a piece of sugar. He was forced to mix with a spoon disproportionately large for the small cup.

"Ah, the French!" he said. "Could that be the same nation who developed the metric system in 1799?"

A table near the window would be a great place to kill some time until his appointment with Dr. Udayasekaran. But he would have had to endure hearing a car alarm from outside. He chose to sit in a comfortable chair in front of the television. The voice of the TV program's host covered all the noise.

He watched the program for five minutes without paying attention, without really understanding what it is about. An old lady was telling a story, apparently a sad one. She had rather a strange accent. After a few words, she shed tears. Then someone else appeared. A young man. He also had a slight accent but spoke better than the last. There was anger in his voice. Hayri did not understand what he said and did not care. -

Suddenly he thought he heard the word 'Turk' at the TV. He concentrated himself to listen but a group of chattering nurses entered the cafeteria. They were here for a coffee break.

He rose from his and approached the TV, to hear the words. At that moment, he felt the vibration of the BlackBerry in his pocket. The display was indicating that this was his mother.

"Hi mom? How are you doing?"

Her trembling voice made him understand that there was something that was not right. She was speaking too fast.

"Mom, I'm in a noisy place. Wait, until I go some to place silent."

His mother continued to talk without listening. Hayri walked out, away from the noise, seeking a corner as quiet as possible. This seemed a difficult task at this hour, in the corridors of the hospital. Finally he found a quiet corner and had her repeat his words several times.

He finally understood. His aunt in Istanbul was ill, in the hospital. The doctors had decided to operate her in the heart and his mother wanted immediately to leave for Istanbul, early tomorrow morning, to be near her sister during the operation. She also asked if he could hold on during her absence. That comment made Hayri smile. Would his mother have forgotten so quickly that her son had been single last couple of years, before both have decided to go together to Paris?

After trying to calm his mother, he promised to accompany her tomorrow to the airport, then he hung up. He could not help thinking that after the departure of his mother, a lonely life would begin again.

Thoughtfully, he approached a window turned into a mirror because of the gray sky. He needed to look out. Instead of a Parisian landscape, he could see nothing but his own reflection similar to a shadow. Behind his shadow, he noticed another one. It should be the visual effect of the double glass installed to reduce the heat loss.

But strange! The double of his shadow was making different movements, independent of his.

He suddenly whirled to meet a man a few steps behind him. It was someone who had a cell phone to the ear. He was speaking in a low voice, or pretending to speak. When their eyes met, the man briskly turned to walk down the hallway.

How could he come so near Hayri without being noticed? This man, could he be one of the followers mentioned by Sinan Bey?

Was there real danger to him? And these men, why were they following him? Maybe it would be safer to return to Turkey? He was overwhelmed by both fear and anger. Now he was becoming paranoid.

The word 'paranoid' took his thoughts to Rashad, to his old friend from Diyarbakir and from French school in Istanbul. During his college years, he had met Rashad again in Ankara. They had even shared the same room at the campus. But his old friend had changed, he was no longer the same boy. He was now a paranoid schizophrenic. He was believing that he was being followed all the time by enemies, aliens and other things.

Was Hayri becoming like him?

***

Sixth session

“Why did you refuse the scholarship for your graduate studies in France?” asked Nadir.

“I already told you. I had no desire to return to the country where my father was murdered.”

The silence that followed those words lasted nearly a minute. Nadir tried to say something but gave up, leaving the floor to Hayri.

Finally Hayri continued his story:

“After I have got my high school diploma in Istanbul, I was settled in Ankara, with my mother. But this comfort lasted only for a few months because my mother retired and moved to Istanbul to live with her sister.”

But he did say that already to Nadir. Why was he repeating the same words? Could that be because he was not ready yet to tell the main story?

He remained thoughtful for a few moments. His mother was doing exactly the same thing, today. For a mother, could a sister be more important than a son?

A glance at Nadir made him understand that the doctor was waiting patiently for him to speak.

“Instead of moving to an apartment and do housework, I decided to move to the campus. The campus was about twenty miles away from the city center. Along with two friends from Istanbul, I planned to share a room at the campus dormitory. But at the last moment they changed their minds. The parents of one of them decided to move to Ankara. Naturally, he would live with them. The second got married and went to the United States. Again, I found myself alone," said Hayri, smiling.

Nadir returned his smile.

"So, what did you do?" he asked.

"The best solution for me was still the same: I would move to the campus. Management gave me a choice of rooms. The one at the first floor seemed the most convenient. So I decided to see it. All my stuff was in a suitcase. I could settle immediately.

The campus rules were prohibiting the locking the doors of the room. To enter, I all I had to do was to push the door with my shoulder. In the room, a boy, standing before a table, was reading a magazine. He seemed extremely focused on what he was watching. I could only see him from behind. He did not hear me entering. While I was looking for a way to signal my presence in the room, I was frozen in place by what I saw. The guy had dropped his pants and was masturbating while looking at pictures of naked women in the magazine!"

"Funny way to meet for the first time a roommate," said Nadir, keeping a straight face.

Obviously this was an unnecessary detail. Hayri should have skipped that.

"I threw my suitcase on the bed and walked out. I immediately understood that it would not be easy for me to share a room with people I do not know. I made a little walk around to see the other rooms. None of them was located as convenient as the first one."

"When I was back in the room, an hour later, I haven't seen anyone. The room for four people and there were four narrow lockers. Two of them were open and empty. The other two were locked. So there was a third person in the room other than me and the 'masturbator'. And the fourth was still missing.

Yawning of his interlocutor made Hayri understand that he was entering into too much detail. Or, Nadir was not in the mood today.

He looked at his watch, it was time to leave. I didn't want to miss his appointment with Esther.

***

"St Georges Street at 9th arrondissement" he told the driver, after checking the address.

The taxi drove off. It was late afternoon and traffic was blocking almost all boulevards. But the driver who knew how to choose favorable low traffic streets. In less than twenty minutes, they arrived at the destination.

Getting out of the taxi, he looked at his watch. He had not missed the appointment. He could read the name of the restaurant: Chez Ara.

The notes of a familiar music filtering through the door, surprised him. Once inside he could hear the words of a popular song, though did not know the meaning.

Soudeh, soudeh, soudeh, amehn pahn soudeh
Ays askharhin vourrah, amehn pahn soudeh[70]

A voice called:

"Hayri!"

This was Esther. She was waving her hand to him. He approached the table where she was already seated. With a big smile, she raised her glass in the form of greeting:

"While waiting for you, I had a glass of wine."

"Am I late?" asked Hayri, looking at his watch.

"No, not at all," she replied, still smiling.

She should have taken more than one glass and she looked prettier than the last time he saw her. When was the last time he had slept with a woman?

To hide obscene ideas, he buried his head into the menu. All meals looked delicious but they had less than an hour to eat. They should hurry.

***

At this hour, it was a miracle to find a spot to park the car near the Théâtre du Palais-Royal. After several rounds in the streets around the theater, they finally came across someone who was leaving. Esther surprised Hayri by her parallel parking ability between two cars.

Despite all the efforts, they were late. The attendant told them she could let them in only during the entr'acte, showing them the armchairs of the lobby.

"Do you know the story of Esther?" asked Esther.

---

[70] Armenian popular song:

False, false, false everything is false.
In this world everything is false

Hayri realized that a typical intellectual conversation was about to start. It was a shame that he never took the time to read the little book he had purchased.

"No," he said. "When I was in high school in Istanbul, we studied *Phèdre* in French Literature class but not *Esther*."

She smiled, showing her whitened teeth. Despite all the wine she had drunk, she seemed sober, more sober than Hayri anyway,

"Esther is my name, you know."

She must have already figured out that his companion had difficulty in grasping the names. Hayri felt the heat on his ears and began to blush. He had never been a good liar, especially when talking to women. Being aware of his 'disability', how could he even accept a diplomatic mission in Paris?

"I can give you a summary of this work of Racine. It would be easier for you to follow the play," said Esther.

"If you want, said Hayri," a little tense.

Then she told him the exciting story of Esther, and Hayri listened without interrupting. She was a good storyteller.

When she finally finished her story, the audience began to leave the room for the entr'acte. The usher beckoned them to approach. They arose.

"Thanks for telling me the story of Esther," said Hayri. "But you have not told me why you two 'heroines' have the same name?

The usher showed them their place. They sat down.

“Thank you for qualifying me as ‘heroine’,” she said, still with her beautiful smile.

She continued talking, looking straight into Hayri’s eyes.

“When I was born, mother gave me that name. She told me that her mother, this means my grandmother, that I have ever seen, had a neighbor in Heidelberg before the war. This neighbor had a daughter named Esther. My mother and Esther were best friends.

After the ‘gong’ sound, the audience were returning to their seats. The second act was about to start.

“One day the Gestapo came to take them.”

The room plunged into darkness. She continued to talk in whispers:

“After the war, my mother waited for the return of her girlfriend with hope but she never returned. My mother decided that when she would grow up if she had a daughter, she would give her the name of the missing girlfriend. My name was decided long before my birth”

The curtain opened. Ester approached the ear Hayri to tell him:

“You and I, we belong to two great nations who have committed two big crimes of the world history.”

“Speak for yourself!” said Hayri, with an angry voice.

“Silence!” said someone in from the audience.

***

He had thought of walking out the theater at once but a diplomat would never do such a rude thing, especially to a woman.

And later, why did he accepted the invitation of Esther to go to her apartment? Of course, it was just for a coffee. But it's always for a coffee, isn't it?

Hayri had no thought of bringing up the same subject: 'the great crimes of the history.' This wouldn't be subject he could discuss without losing his temper and he would probably start to stutter.

They did not exchange a single word during the short drive in Esther's car. She was living in an apartment near the Eiffel Tower. They entered into the garage in the basement. The elevator took them to the fifth floor. The living room window gave them a great view. He was amazed by the Eiffel Tower's sparkling lights.

"The rent must cost you a fortune," he said, as if it was his concern.

In response, she only smiled. She approached the American bar, while Hayri was savoring the magnificent view.

"Do you really want a coffee? Or can I get you something better?" asked Esther.

"I could have a Scotch on the rocks," he said, thinking that alcohol would help him to relax.

She put the ice with her hand, poured the whiskey and put the glass on the coffee table in front of Hayri.

"Would you be angry with me for what I told you at the theater?" she asked.

The heart of Hayri began to beat strongly. This woman had her methods to open sensitive topics.

“No, he answered. But why waste a night like this, speaking of events that happened almost a century ago?”

“Ah!” she said. “I always forget how the Turks are susceptible to that matter.”

“Susceptible!?” asked Hayri. His voice was raised involuntarily.

The silence that followed a few seconds seemed like hours. Hayri felt the need to start over, but this time he tried a soft tone:

“Do you know that I am the son of a Turkish diplomat murdered by...”

“By fanatic assassins? Yes,” she said.

This time the silence was heavier and longer.

Finally she spoke again:

“I am truly sorry for your father.”

Hayri did not answer. He felt that if he tried to speak, he would definitely stutter.

“Revenge is the weapon of the downtrodden,” she said.

What was she trying to say? She was not only a psychologist but also a philosopher, perhaps?

“This is a quote from Alice Brunel-Roche[71],” she said, to explain.

Finally Hayri exploded:

“Esther!” he said. “You do not understand! You can’t co ... co ... compare ...”

[71] From: *LA HAINE ENTRE LES DENTS.*

He paused. The stutter was coming back and it was worse than a nightmare. He breathed deeply tried again:

“The Germans, are they looking for an apology, or perhaps even ac ... ac ... accomplices to their big sin?”

A glazed look invaded the eyes of Esther, which was quickly masked by a smile.

“You know?” she said, “You are very different from the Turks I have known in Germany. They are almost all brown and have dark looks that don’t like.”

What game was she playing again? It was a mistake for Hayri to come to her apartment. He stood up and walked towards the door. But she quickly stepped forward to stand between him and door.

The exit was blocked. Hayri shocked, did not know what to do.

She spoke softly, putting her arms around his neck:

“But unlike the other Turks I knew, you are handsome. And when you're angry, you become way too sexy.”

“I...”

IX

These 'tourist' families, with their children, and maps in their pockets, were in search of the treasures of their grandfathers and their grandmothers...

Levent Dincer[72]

The tourist

It took him a few seconds to realize that he was not in his own bed. The need to go to the toilet forced him to rise. He left the room. Where could the bathroom be?

He went to a window. The lights of the Eiffel Tower were off. What time could it be? ...

He finally found the door to the bathroom in the dark and entered. Groping, he found the switch and pressed. A blinding fluorescent light flashed. When

[72] From the book titled: Beret and Scarf.

his eyes adjusted to the light, he was surprised by his own image in the mirror. He was naked! He gave himself a mischievous smile. He had bedded that German woman.

Ah! It was difficult to start urinating. Was it because he was getting old, already? His mother must be curious, rather worried to know where her son was spending the night.

Worried? But!?...

As soon as he was done, he returned to the room running. The noise he made woke Esther.

"What happened?" she asked.

He explained he had completely forgotten that his mother was going to take the plane to Istanbul today and he had promised to take her to the airport. She was probably very worried now that his son did not return home the night before her travel.

The dead battery of the BlackBerry had totally isolated him from the rest of the world. He searched for his clothes scattered here and there. Again, he had been irresponsible.

"Could you call a taxi for me please? I have to go home quick," he said to Esther, who was sitting in the bed and looking him with surprise.

"I do not know if you can get one right away," she said, jumping out of bed.

Her naked body was enjoyable to watch. Despite his haste, Hayri could not pass without noticing this. She began to dress quickly.

"You do not need to bother for me," he said.

"I do not want you to have problems with your mother because of me, she said. I'll drive you home and to the airport.

"No, I..."

"Shut up!" she said, in a commanding tone. It is not even 5am yet and this hour, you have no chance to find a taxi. So I will drive you. No objections please!

***

The garage door opened and the Volkswagen Eos launched into the street like an arrow. They began to run at high speed. She was driving like a Formula 1 pilot of Le Mans[73].

Hayri had to admit that this woman, this German lady, that is to say Esther, was continuing to impress him at every opportunity.

In less than fifteen minutes of ride, they arrived at his home without incident. A car leaving a parking spot ceded its place. They were lucky.

"I'll wait here," she said.

"No!" said Hayri. "We have time. Please come with me. I want you to meet my mother.

***

During their road trip to Charles de Gaulle, Mrs. Alpergun never stopped talking with Esther.

[73] Le Mans: French 'Daytona' where are races are done.

When passing through passport control, she made them a sign of farewell with a cheerful smile. Would she have accepted already the new girlfriend of her son as the future daughter in law?

When she disappeared from view, Esther took Hayri by the hand and showed him Starbucks.

“Shall we have our breakfast here?”

The touch of her hand was nice. Hayri squeezed it.

“Great idea!” he said.

While they were drinking their coffee and eating their croissants, Hayri had the impression of being watched by one of the customers. This was a little man sitting in a corner. He was throwing furtive glances towards them.

This made Hayri first nervous. Was he becoming paranoid, again?

But he realized with satisfaction that he did not care. He leaned over and gave Esther a kiss on the lips. Then turned his head toward the little man and gave him a wink accompanied by a smile. The man stood up immediately and walked away.

***

On their way back, Hayri was hoping to be invited to her apartment but Esther had other plans.

“Today,” she said, “I will make a presentation at the German Consulate. I need to make some preparations before the conference.”

“Oh? What is the subject?”

“Would you like to come?” asked Esther.

“To the conference? I do not know…”

“There will be a cocktail at the end of the conference. After the cocktail we can go to dinner together, if you want.”

Hayri pretended to think. He wanted to enjoy that moment. Being invited to dinner by a woman wasn’t always the case. Apparently, she was also ‘satisfied’ of the last night.

“Okay,” he said, finally.

“It starts at five o'clock,” she said. “You can take the subway. I will inform the concierge. All you need to do is to give your name at the entrance.”

“I'll be there.”

***

Turning the key to his apartment, he heard the phone ringing. He just had time to pick it up before the person at the other end gave up.

This was Sinan Bey. He wasn’t hiding his anger.

“Where were you last night?”

Hayri would not miss the opportunity for an ironic response:

“Here you surprise me Sinan Bey. I thought the men you put at my back would inform you about everything. Didn’t they do their job?”

“What have done with your cell phone?”

Hayri explained that he had noticed that the battery was low, but he did not bother to recharge. And this morning, he had taken his mother to the airport. She was now on her way to Istanbul.

Sinan Bey said proudly he knew that already. His 'men' had spotted him at Charles de Gaulle Airport.

"Congratulations," said Hayri always ironic. "May I ask what do you want from me, now?"

"Do you always see this German woman?"

This question shocked Hayri.

"Excuse me? It's none of your business!"

Yesterday, the men of Sinan Bey had probably lost his track while he was in the taxi going to the restaurant to meet Esther. And now he was being smart to ask skillfully to know where he had spent the night.

"Remember the words of a wise teacher," said Sinan Bey: 'Beware of women!' And this "fräulein[74]" can be dangerous for you."

"Did you say dangerous? But I know about 'dangerous women' Sinan Bey. Remember? One of them had been my wife!"

There has been a moment of silence. Sinan Bey was probably taken aback. He must have noticed the unusual behavior of his old friend. He changed the tone of his voice:

"All I want is to make sure that you are safe and everything goes well with you."

"Everything is all right Sinan Bey, thank you," said Hayri, in dry voice.

[74] Fräulein (German): Young lady, miss.

But he began to wonder if he had gone too far. Why was he hurting an old friend? After all, the poor man was trying to do his job. He tried to save the situation:

“Are we going to have dinner in a Turkish restaurant, one of these days?”

“In a few days.”

There was another silence. Then Sinan Bey asked:

“Now that your mother is gone, what are you going to do?”

“As I'm alone now, I will become a tourist in Paris.”

Sinan Bey had a laugh:

“Since the accident, mon cher, you already mutated into a tourist!”

***

Seventh session

“You look different today,” said Nadir.

“Different? In what way?” asked Hayri.

“You look happy and relaxed. Something good must have happened with you yesterday.”

Hayri answered only by a big smile.

“Let's go back,” said Nadir. “So, who was your other room buddy in the dormitory? Another masturbator?”

"No," said Hayri smiling. "After observing them for a few weeks, I have decided that my two roommates were actually nice guys and I would have no problems with them."

"And you were relieved?"

"Yes, until the arrival of, guess who?"

His grin made it clear to Nadir he was starting the most important part of his story. He savored a moment the curious gaze of the doctor and finally spoke:

"Three weeks after the start of the fall semester, the fourth guy came to settle in the room. My surprise was great, because this was someone I knew."

He remained thoughtful for a moment. Then continued to talk:

"It was Rashad! My old friend from French high school in Istanbul and from Diyarbakir."

"So, you meet again," said Nadir with a large smile. As if he was expecting that.

Hayri, returned to thc story:

"This was my sophomorc year in college and it was rather a difficult one. Aysel told me about her great idea of continuing her studies in the United States. There was no way I could follow her. She was accepted by Yale and she left a couple of months later. Away from Aysel, I was really alone. Even my mother was away, in Istanbul. Meeting again an old acquaintance Rashad, kept me safe from the idea of being abandoned. Rashad did not give much explanation of his sudden disappearance when we were in high school. I did not insist. I knew him well enough to know he would become even more discreet if tried to question him. He made me understand that he had been in hospital for a period. He gave no reason. He said he was cured. However, he was still a little bizarre, worse than he had been in high school."

"Bizarre? How?" asked Nadir.

Hayri smiled.

"He had no friends other than me. He had already made a reputation in the math class with his genius. I also heard that his teacher of Abstract Mathematics told him not to attend the class because he was too strong compared to other students and would have an 'A' anyway with no problem.

"Did he always believe in telepathy?"

The surprise was big for Hayri.

"How did you know that?"

"I know my job," said Nadir. "Would you please go on? I'm curious about the rest of the story."

His face was reflecting real curiosity. Hayri did not keep him waiting:

"Knowing that someone was trying to get into my brain again was enough to make me crazy. However, my curiosity was stronger. He wanted me to give shot. He would prove that he could read my thoughts and even inject his own ideas into my brain. He would help me in my next math exam."

"How?"

"He would sit on the stairs outside of the building where the exam would take place. I would read him the questions 'telepathically' and he would send me the answers.

He stopped there and looked Nadir silently for a few seconds. Then asked him a question, with the naivety of a child:

"Let's forget about what we said before. Just tell me frankly doctor, do you really believe in telepathy?"

Nadir, who was not expecting this question, did not hide his surprise. He thought for a bit before attempting an answering. Finally he said:

"Good question. It is not in parapsychology that I got my PhD."

Hayri felt he had cornered him. He wanted to go through.

"So you don't really believe it?"

"I did not say that."

There was silence, again. The facial expression of Nadir, made it clear he was trying to find a suitable answer.

"Do you believe in reincarnation?" he asked finally.

It was Hayri's turn to be surprised now. He shrugged his shoulders as a sign of 'I do not know.'

Nadir, satisfied to regain control, asked:

"You know what I mean?"

"No," said Hayri.

Nadir began to walk up and down the room, then suddenly stopped in front of Hayri. He leaned toward him. Their faces were almost touching. He spoke slowly:

"My friend, the Science believes only in things it is capable of explaining."

He had already said that the other day.

Than he straightened. He continued to observe Hayri carefully.

“What did you get?” he asked.

Hayri, did not understand the question:

“What do you mean?”

“I ask what score did you got in the exam!” said Nadir impatiently.

He had got an ‘A’. This was a grade he never had in math before. He decided to ask him a question in return, rather than giving a straight answer:

“Why did you mention about reincarnation, doctor? I do not see the relation.”

“Do you have any idea how many people believe that after their death, they will return to this world?”

Hayri wasn’t sure what to say. But he knew that the population of India was exceeding one billion.

“About ten years ago, I met a doctor at the Ganges shore, said Nadir. His mission was to make the countrymen aware of contagious diseases. Yet he did not hesitate to wash himself in dirty but sacred waters of the river.”

That's where he was going.

“Will you continue with your story, please?” He said to Hayri.

Hayri remembered that he was invited to a conference. He looked at his watch.

“Can I continue tomorrow? I have an appointment.”

He was about to get up but Nadir made him sign to sit.

“You did not tell to me about your nightmares. Does this ‘thing’ still bother you?”

Hayri saw no problem telling the truth.

“Last night, I was with a girlfriend.”

Nadir raised his hand to stop him.

“Okay, I understand,” he said. “This also explains your happy appearance today.”

Hayri tried to hide his blushing by looking at his watch.

“I'm glad you feel good,” said Nadir. “But I'm not sure if this ‘thing’ is really gone forever, or if it is hiding somewhere to return in unexpected moment.”

“What can I do?”

“I want to make sure. Tonight try to sleep ‘alone’ and do not take sleeping pills. Let’s see what happens.”

Alone? This man! Who does he think he is?

“But!” said Hayri.

“Do not be angry,” said the doctor. “You and me, we have to force this thing come out of its hole.”

“?”

“And make it disappear completely.”

"But I do not understand, said Hayri. Why to wake it up? And if it comes back, what shall I do?"

"I think if we work together, we can get it back. And when you feel that it is behind you, I mean in your dream, you'll just have to take an action."

"What action?" asked Hayri, confused.

"You are going turn your head back and look at it."

"But, you know that I can't!"

"You must make an effort. If you manage to look back, you'll see that it will disappear."

Hayri was more confused than ever. He stood up and walked to the door. Before opening it, he turned his head slowly to look back to Nadir, as if he was practicing what he was just told to do.

"And so it will disappear completely from my life?" he said, trying an ironic tone.

"Just like Eurydice," said Nadir.

"To do that, I am going to have to sleep on your inclined chair? But I can only sleep in my own bed."

"I think it's time to talk about hypnosis."

"What?"

"Do not panic Hayri. Hypnosis could be a successful method in cases like yours."

Hayri, moved away from the door and went to sit on a chair.

“Mr. Udayasekaran. We talked about telepathy, reincarnation and now we talk about hypnosis? Today, you are really surprising me. Do you really want to make me sleep here?”

“I'm pretty good at hypnosis. But if you want, we could also have the help of a friend expert on this.”

Hayri gestured ‘no’ with his hand.

“I think we went too far with this therapy. I do not want to see a third person for hypnosis or any other method.”

Nadir approached him and put his hand on his shoulder.

“This thing may never leave you alone. I met this problem before with some of my patients. This ‘thing’ must be taken out of its hole and disappeared!”

Hayri was puzzled. Was this man normal?

“What would you say for a small test now?” asked Nadir.

“Now? You mean with hypnosis?”

“Let me first explain what hypnosis is: this is an altered state of consciousness. The subject in hypnotic state is more capable of focusing his attention.”

“Is that so?”

“This is a state that we will achieve together. You must be cooperative.”

“Am I going to hypnotize myself?”

“It's not magic, and if you participate, it will be easier for both of us to communicate during your state of hypnosis. So, do you want to make a small test now?”

“Now?”

“Yes, just a small test. It is possible that we do not succeed the first time, but it is worth trying.”

“Actually, I'm curious to try it,” said Hayri. “But I must admit that this scares me a little.”

“I understand. As I say, this will be just a small test. I promise not to push the limits. Moreover, you can stop whenever you want.”

“Really? But I thought...”

“As I said, I am not a natural hypnotist. I learned this technique long after having my PhD and I only use it to communicate with my patients.”

“Well then, let's try,” said Hayri. “But wake me in ten minutes, please. Because I have a meeting at five o'clock.”

“With a beautiful woman, I suppose,” said Nadir, with a big smile showing his white teeth.

Then he opened his desk drawer to get out of a red silk scarf.

“Lay on your back and cover your eyes with this, pointing to the inclined ‘dentist's’ chair”.

“Why do you want to cover my eyes, doctor?”

“Trust me,” said Nadir.

Hayri wondered if he would abandon the idea about hypnosis and escape from the room where everything was red. Or try a new experience?

He followed the instructions of the Nadir. What would Sinan Bey say if he knew that Hayri was trying hypnosis?

***

The rain caught him at the subway exit. Yet half an hour earlier, the sun was shining in a blue sky. As usual, he had no umbrella. He had lost a couple of expensive ones before deciding not to bother carrying one.

During ten minute walk in the rain he did not stop thinking about his unique experience with hypnosis. With the help of Nadir, he had observed that the 'thing' was still there, waiting for an opportunity to harass him.

When he arrived at the door of the Consulate, he was all wet. The hostess at the front desk ushered him into a room and showed him an electric iron specially made for pants. Hayri had seen similar one in a hotel in London. She also offered him a hairdryer to dry his shirt.

Fifteen minutes later he was back at the reception desk. He had missed first half an hour of the presentation.

He read the sign posted on an easel:

"THE STAGES OF GRIEF"
Speaker:
Esther BAUER, Ph.D.
University of Heidelberg

Another hostess pinned him on the still wet jacket the name label: *Hayrettin Alpergun*. Esther had kept her promise. They were was expecting him.

When he entered, the room was dark. A third hostess helped him sit by making the sign of "hush!"

On the stage, Esther was speaking before a screen where a PowerPoint presentation was projected.

From the tone of her voice, it was easy to observe that she was sure of herself.

"This was Dr. Elisabeth Kübler-Ross who first put forward the idea of the 'stages of grief'. These stages can be applied to any form of catastrophic loss. Dr. Kübler-Ross model has five stages; the first one is the 'denial'.

Eyes accustomed to the dark, he looked around. There was a cosmopolitan audience. All seats were occupied. Although the speech was in French, she was giving the English translation of important technical expressions. Hayri tried to concentrate.

"For example," she said, "during the denial stage, the sufferer will react. He or she will say: *But is it possible? They must to be wrong! Such a thing can't happen to me*."

"When he/she finally understands that this is true, the second step will start: the 'anger'. *Why me? Not others? It's unfair!*

She gave a pleasant smile to the audience; as if she was talking about a love story but not a disaster. She looked very feminine on the stage, like a movie actress.

"And then comes the third stage which is 'bargaining'. For example, the sufferers can try to bargain with God: *I will do everything you want. Take my life, but let my son live.*"

Someone in the room raised his hand to ask a question:

“Are these reactions the same in everyone?”

Esther answered in soft voice:

“You can see variations from one person to another. You can also see variations from one nation to another; or rather from one culture to another.”

A murmur ran through the audience. Esther explained:

“Let’s compare for example the people of Europe; those who live in the north and the south. For Swedes, if something is not going well, it is always their own fault. You can even see them suiciding for ‘their’ fault. But for a Sicilian, in case of a similar situation, it is always someone else’s fault. A Sicilian might even consider killing the 'guilty' person.”

The murmur grew in the room. Other people raised their hands to ask questions.

Hayri had enough. He left the room, especially because of the need to relieve his bladder. He began to look for the toilet. The voice of Esther could still be heard, but fading as he walked away.

He opened a door which gave access to another room. Waiters dressed in white, were preparing a long table, apparently for the cocktail that would follow the conference.

He closed the door and turned. There was a man behind him: a bearded man with gray hair. He wore a bow tie.

“I bet you are looking for the restroom, like me,” he said with a smile.

They had to go to the entrance of the building to ask the guard where the toilet was. Their journey ended at the second floor, and when they finally began to urinate alongside, a usual male bathroom conversation began between the two men:

“More I get older, more I frequent the toilet,” said the bearded man.

He was looking like an artist, a painter or something like that.

“Have you heard about these principles?” asked Hayri, just to have a conversation.

“Principles? What principles?” said the bearded man with a surprise that seemed sincere.

“I mean the stages of grief.”

“Ah!” said the bearded man. “I am in the final stage: the acceptance”.

What was he trying to say? Hayri pulled the zipper of his pants and went to the sink to wash his hands. The bearded man joined him.

“I have cancer and I went through all these stages,” he said.

Hayri, having no desire to hear the rest, hurried out into the corridor. But the bearded man followed him.

“And finally I accepted,” said the man.

They walked down the stairs. Hayri’s companion had no intention to leave him.

“I am a professor of philosophy,” he said. “Frau Bauer and I are old friends.”

Arrived on the first floor, they noticed that the doors of the conference room were wide open. People in groups were entering to the cocktail lounge.

A man approached his companion:

“Herr Professor!”

They began a conversation in German. This gave Hayri the opportunity get away. Esther was surrounded by several people. He preferred to leave her with them for now. A woman approached him to read his name on his chest then turned her look into his eyes.

“You're Turkish,” she said.

Hayri gestured with his head ‘yes’. He had no desire to cling to another person, but it was a place where he was supposed to be polite. After all, wasn’t he a diplomat who had studied all the rules of politeness?

“Are you also a professor?” he asked with his best smile.

“No,” said the woman. “I am a journalist.”

“Oh, really?”

This was the last thing he needed; a journalist.

“Since you are Turkish, I would like to speak with you on the Kurdish Rebellion,” she said.

And now, it was starting ‘well’. As a diplomat, he was more or less prepared for all kind of embarrassing questions. But today, he had no desire to talk about «boring» subjects, especially those a French journalist would be interested.

Quick! He needs a diversion.

“Do you know about the Venn circles, by any chance?” he asked, as if he was speaking of a serious thing.

“No?” she said with an obvious surprise.

“Do you know why you do not know?”

She seemed more surprised. Hayri grimaced:

“I bet you don’t know about Boolean Equations either. Then you would not understand anything of I tell you. In this case, it is not worth talking about.”

She totally freaked out. Satisfied with his weird victory, Hayri walked away with a large smile. What he did, was not polite but she was deserving that. Asking political questions that had nothing to do with the conference was not appropriate.

He saw Esther in a corner, still surrounded by the men and women of her audience. Apparently, the conference was very successful. An excited conversation was going on. This wasn’t a good time to approach her. He fell back on the buffet full of delicious things and grabbed a plate.

A hand touched his shoulder. He turned his head thinking that it was the annoying journalist.

It was Esther. Her lipstick was a fiery red.

“Come on,” she said.” I want to introduce you to my friends.”

Damn! Said Hayri, quietly. But it was impossible to refuse. He nodded his head in agreement, like a little shy boy.

* * *

Conversations with intellectuals were far from being interesting. When all was finished, his watch was showing 8pm.

And the French journalist that he avoided earlier, had cornered him.

"I think t*he Turks have passed the stage of denial*," she had said. "*They are now at the stage of anger*."

And suddenly, Hayri had lost his composure.

"Ah! You French," he had said, "*You think you are the gift of God to humanity!*"

Could that be the words of a diplomat? No! But the fuse of his patience had blown.

It was the hope to spend the rest of the night with Esther that had forced him to wait until the end of the cocktail. But alas, she had a headache. On the way back, in the taxi, she began to cough. Arrived in front of her apartment, Hayri had to refuse her invitation politely.

"I'll call you tomorrow," he said. "You must have caught cold. Go to bed early and sleep well."

Esther gave him a friendly wave when entering the building but she looked exhausted.

***

Hayri was disappointed. He was planning to talk to her. As a psychologist, she could give him her professional opinion on therapeutic hypnosis.

This experience was still nagging his mind. When Nadir gradually put him under hypnosis, he had felt the presence of the thing. This 'thing' he thought was disappeared…

He was afraid, too afraid. More afraid than his nightmares. Nadir had to stop the session.

He had fled the room promising to return tomorrow without being sure if he would have the courage to keep his promise. Tonight, he would not fail to take a sleeping pill. Maybe even two...

"Where are we going, monsieur?"

This was the driver. Deep in thought, he forgot he was still in a taxi.

"Rue Palatine, 6th arrondissement, please madame," he said.

The driver was a woman of a certain age. Why the word 'chauffeur[75]' had no female form, like most of the other words of French?

She had a dog, a German shepherd, sat quietly beside her. How come he had not noticed him before getting into the taxi?

Leaning his head against the window, he tried in vain to plunge into dreams. But he could not concentrate. The taxi rolled on the banks of the Seine at a speed that seemed excessive. Outside, the 'city of light' was shining in all its splendor.

"I've changed my mind," he said, suddenly. "Could you take me to the Pont des Arts, please?"

"Of course, monsieur."

---

[75] driver

Fifteen minutes later, he got out of the taxi. The weather was getting cold and there was no body on the bridge Pont des Art. Now, he had to walk two or three kilometers up to his home. But in Paris, a good walk, had always been his best occupation.

X

There are forty or fifty emaciated ***phantoms*** *crowded into the compound opposite our school. They are women out of their mind; they have forgotten how to eat; when one offers them bread, they throw it aside with indifference. They only groan and wait for death*[76]*.*

The stages of grief

This time, it was the BlackBerry that awoke him. While stretching himself, he felt he was in good mood. He pressed the button to answer. This was his mother.

"Hayri, my son, how are you?"

"I was going to call you, mom. I'm fine. How is my aunt?"

"She just came out of surgery room. The doctor says she's going to be okay."

[76] Excerpt from the letter dated October 8, 1915 signed by four professors from German School in Aleppo of the Ottoman Empire, to the Ministry of Foreign Affairs in Berlin.

“Ah! I'm glad to hear that. How about you? Are you okay too?”

“Yes, yes I'm fine. But it bothers me for leaving you alone out there. What do you eat now?”

Ah, moms! Always worried about their children.

“I'm old enough, mom. Please stop worrying about me. I can take care of myself.”

“Yes, I know. I have to stay here a few more weeks, until your aunt recovers.”

“No problem, mom. Do not forget to tell my aunt that I wish her a good recovery.”

“I will not fail. Goodbye. I kiss you my son.”

“Goodbye Mom. I kiss you both.”

He looked at his watch hanging up and was surprised to see it was already 10:30am. He had forgotten to set his alarm clock. The double dose of sleeping pills had definitely made their job. There was no nightmare. On the other side, he woke much later than he was expecting.

His appointment with Nadir was at 11:30. He jumped out of bed and began to dress. The battery of the BlackBerry was almost dead, as usual. It was fortunate that the conversation with his mother was not interrupted. He plugged it immediately to let it charge while he ate his breakfast.

Fifteen minutes later he was in the street.

***

Eighth session

“So, are you ready for hypnosis, today?” asked Nadir.

“Yes, I am. I'm sorry about yesterday. I was scared, so scared. I was feeling the breath of this ‘thing’ on my neck.”

“But you didn’t try to look at it, did you?”

“I was so curious, but you know that I still can’t turn my head back.”

“You do not have a sore neck but it seems the psychological effects of your accident are still there.”

Was there a little irony in his words?

“Well, said Hayri. Let's try again.”

He lay on his back and closed his eyes.

“You need to make an effort, said Nadir. I already told you that hypnosis is something that we will achieve together. Trust me. And if this “thing” shows up again, do not panic. Just let me know that it is there behind you. I am going to help you turn your head to see it. In dreams, a lot of people can’t turn their head to look back. They can’t run either, to escape a danger. So, you are not the only one who is facing this problem. But with me, you are not alone. I am going to help you.”

These words seemed to comfort Hayri. He closed his eyes.

“I want you to put the veil on your face again,” said Nadir.

Hayri obeyed without objection.

***

Hypnosis

"Mayrig![77] Someone is knocking the door!"

"Go, open it Eurydice."

Eurydice ran to the window and leaned dangerously out. She gave a cry of joy when she saw her grandfather and her father.

There were two men with them. Looked like two soldiers. Her grandfather had probably invited them for lunch.

Yet, it was still too early for lunch. Besides, why her dad was also with them? But the store? Who was taking care of the customers? Usually his grandfather would not shut the store before the sunset. It was too early.

Again there was a knock at the door. A little louder this time.

"Open the door!" said an impatient voice.

This was not the voice of her father, nor grandfather. This should be one of the guests. "He must be very hungry," thought Eurydice.

Down the stairs she saw her mother walking out of the kitchen. Her hands were white of flour. She looked anxious.

"It's dad and grandfather. They have guests," said Eurydice, to calm her down.

But words were not enough to calm her. Because the young woman had heard rumors. She had heard that the soldiers were knocking at the doors and telling people to collect their belongings and prepare for a long trip.

[77] Mayrig (Armenian): Mother.

There has been third knock. This one was really loud. Eurydice froze behind the door. She looked at the horrified face of her mother with surprise.

They heard the soft voice of the grandfather:

"Come open the door, Eurydice. There is no reason to be afraid."

The little girl opened the door. Four men took their shoes off and entered the house.

One of the soldiers said something to grandfather. Eurydice did not understand. Her grandfather explained:

"Our country is on war and our government has issued an order to move us elsewhere for security reasons. Your father and I have already evacuated the store and installed our stuff on the carriage. I'm going to the barn to prepare the other carriage. Start to pack your luggage with your mom."

One of the soldiers asked if there were other people in the house. Grandfather showed him the stairs. The soldier went upstairs to take a glance and went down quickly.

"Do not forget. At noon!" he told to the grandfather exiting the house.

The door closed, there was silence. Family members looked at each other. Apart Eurydice, they all knew what all these meant. A minute later, they heard one of the soldiers calling grandfather to come out:

"Gevorg efendi[78]*, come here!"*

Grandfather rushed out to see what the soldiers wanted. He closed the door behind him. Eurydice curious, tried to look out the window but saw nothing.

[78] Efendi (Turkish): Mister, sir.

Then she climbed up the stairs and looked out the window of the second floor to see what was going on in the courtyard.

She saw her grandfather and the soldiers entering the barn. They were quick to come out with two horses. One of the soldiers was holding Khar by the bridle, the favorite horse of the family. The grandfather saw Eurydice at window. Usually, every time he saw her, he smiled. But this time his face was expressionless.

The soldiers mounted the horses and went out of the yard.

"Why do they take my horse?" shouted Eurydice.

The old man pretended not to hear and entered the house. The little girl came down the stairs, hoping for an explanation. She missed a step and almost fell. Her father caught her.

All gathered around the grandfather. And grandfather started to speak.

... ...

Mayrig threw the shovel to a corner of the garden, away from the spot where she had buried the tin box wrapped in oiled cloth. One day, would she have the chance to return home and to find her modest jewelry?

The horses the soldiers had left were old. Younger ones were confiscated. She climbed on the carriage, by the side of her father. Her mother had moved in the other carriage with grandfather. They had taken everything that was necessary, or almost everything...

Riding outside the garden gate, Eurydice turned to take a look at her house. Was that the last time she was looking at it?

… …

There were people outside the town hall. Men, women and children... They were all gathered in the square.

A soldier told them that each family was only allowed one carriage. So they put their entire load in one of the carriages. Of course, they had to abandon some of their luggage. The armchair of the grandfather was among them.

The convoy moved. The soldiers were with them. Everyone obeyed. There were no tears, no cries of protest.

For Eurydice, although a little worried, it all sounded like an adventure.

"Where are we going grandfather?" she asked several times. Nobody knew the answer. Even the soldiers who were accompanying the convoy did not know exactly where they were heading to.

… …

They walked for two days and arrived at the foot of a mountain. The soldiers told them to stop there, but did not say why.

The high sun was hot. Mayrig distributed to the family water from the jug that she kept in the shade. The grandfather told Eurydice to shelter under the carriage. She was almost asleep when she began to hear whispers. She came out from under the car to see what was happening. Another convoy was approaching.

"Those are the people from D...," said the grandfather. "They evacuate all villages."

Now they were over a hundred people silently waiting new orders.

This hateful silence was torn by the cry of a woman:

"I want to stay with my husband!"

The officer who commanded the soldiers approached her and spoke quietly:

"We have orders, bacim[79]*. All men between ages fifteen and thirty stays here. Others will move on. They will join you later."*

"But why?" said the woman with tears. "I want to stay with my husband."

The officer walked away without answering.

It took several minutes for others to understand that this order involved everyone in the convoy.

… …

The convoy stopped at an intersection where the road was separating into two. The narrow and stony one, barely a path, was climbing the mountain. The other was going down to the plain, towards the city.

"Perhaps my father will join us here," said Eurydice, hopefully.

Grandfather, face full of sweat, seemed less optimistic. He had noticed that the carriages at the head of the convoy were unloading their luggage. The soldiers were ordered to lead the convoy through the mountain path. They were not supposed to go through the city. They were not supposed to be 'seen'.

Carriages could not go by that route. They had to leave everything here. The rest of the route would be made on foot.

… …

[79] Bacim (Turkish): Sister.

Grandfather laid his burden down and sat on a rock. Eurydice, who had never seen him so tired and worried.

Somehow she was glad of these delays, because his father would able to catch up. She always wanted to believe that he was following. But the soldiers were not happy with delays. The convoy should keep moving.

The grandfather and other old people had been allowed to rest a little, but with the condition that others continued walking.

So, Mayrig and Eurydice let him rest and they continued walking. The father and the grandfather would join them in the next stop

… …

Now, in the convoy, there were only women left. They continued to walk. Mayrig and other women in the convoy knew this was their only chance to survive.

They crossed a mountain village. The people surprised, staring them with the quizzical looks did not understand why those women were here. Where were they going? Nobody knew.

An old woman in the convoy asked for some water to the villagers, but the villagers did not respond. However, they were not kind of people who would take pleasure of others' sufferings. They were only mountain people. They just could not believe their eyes. They had never seen a crowd like that; crowd of women walking through their village. The sight of those 'phantoms' had frozen them. None responded to old woman's begging for water.

Except a little girl of six years plunged his tin cup into the trough and brought water to the old woman who was thirsty.

The old woman thanked her.

… …

The deadly walk continued for weeks still to an unknown destination. Those who remained behind, were still not coming. Even the soldiers had abandoned them.

Eurydice suddenly noticed that Mayrig was no more with her. She looked all around. Her mother was not in sight.

Terrified, she turned around and started to walk fast, shouting: "Mayrig! Mayrig!"

The people she met on her way told her not to walk back but she would not listen.

Finally she saw her mother crouched on the ground. She looked exhausted.

"Walk! Eurydice, walk!" she said. "I'll join you later."

"Mayrig! I'll wait here with you."

"No!" Cried Mayrig. "One of us need to reach the destination. One of us need to survive."

And eyes closed, Eurydice walked; until she became invisible to the eyes of human beings.

***

Hayri opened his eyes and pulled the red veil.

“Are you tired?” asked Nadir.

“No,” he said, getting up from the inclined chair.

But he had to sit down back immediately feeling dizzy.

“So, we can talk a little about the story you just told me?” asked Nadir.

“I told you a story?”

“Of course. Don’t you remember?”

Hayri thought for a bit. He was remembering every detail. It was like he had just seen the fragments of a movie.

“And this little girl named Eurydice, who was she?” asked Nadir.

“What do I know? She came like that, as one of the characters in my movie-dream.”

They looked each other for some time without speaking. Nadir finally walked to his desk, opened a drawer and pulled out a book. He turned the pages looking for something. Hayri stared his facial expressions. The doctor finally heaved a sigh of relief and put his finger on a page.

“The name of this little girl in this story you just told me, reminds me of something. You know the myth of Orpheus and Eurydice, don’t you?”

“I graduated the School of the Brothers. I studied French culture, so, ‘naturally’ I know about Greek mythology,” said Hayri, with a nervous laugh.

“Ah!” Nadir sighed, still smiling.

He seemed to have fun reading this page. Finally, he turned his look to Hayri.

"Stories of Eurydice, they are all sad. You know it is always about a woman who disappeared 'twice'. I even remember a film directed by Marcel Camus: *Black Orpheus*."

Nadir was right. Eurydice disappeared twice in each of her sad stories. And it was always a backward glance which made her disappear.

"I understand but I don't see the relation," said Hayri. "I think the real question is: why and how did I have such a dream? I did not read a book or seen a movie like this, recently."

"Is it possible that you created it yourself, in your mind?"

"Mr. Udayasekaran, I am neither a writer nor a producer. This was more like a movie someone told me, showing some pictures."

Noticing the abrupt change of expression on the face of the doctor, he stopped.

"Someone told you about a movie? Who, for example?" asked Nadir.

Like any lawyer this man obviously knew the art of playing with the words. Hayri preferred to stay silent to avoid falling into a trap.

"And this 'thing', was it always behind you?"

"No, not this time. I did not feel its presence."

"Have you tried to turn your head to look at it?"

"No, I didn't. As I have said, this time everything was quiet. There was nothing that scared me. This was not like a nightmare."

Nadir approached his put his hands on his shoulders.

“But don’t you understand Hayri? This ‘thing’ is like Eurydice and the next time you have a nightmare, turn your head back! You have to look at it. Believe me, it will completely disappear from your life.”

This man had too much imagination. Maybe Hayri had made a mistake by continuing the sessions with him. Maybe he was a little insane. Moreover, psychologists, aren’t they all insane, a little?

“Why?” asked Hayri, trying to hide his anxiety.

“Don’t you see that you need to kill this thing symbolized in Eurydice?”

Hayri looked at the exit. He could reach the door in a second but decided to wait for the right moment.

“Kill?” he said, in a trembling voice.

Nadir corrected immediately:

“I mean ‘look’. This creature that you kept calling ‘thing’ is waiting for your look. This is all it needs. Then it will walk away from your life.”

“I want to go,” said Hayri, heart pounding.

Nadir nodded with disappointment.

“Forgive me”, he said. “I went too fast. I sincerely try to save you from these nightmares. You are a special case for me.”

He took his hands from Hayri’s shoulders and stepped back.

“In a few weeks, I leave Paris. I received an offer for a teaching position in Columbia University in New York. I will move to the New World. But before leaving France, I want to be sure that you're okay.”

Hayri regretted his words. His desire to leave disappeared. Nadir was a good man. Then why was he panicking, all of a sudden?

“Let’s change the subject,” said Nadir. “Are you going to tell me the rest of your college adventures on campus in Ankara?”

“Now?”

The psychologist looked at his watch.

“I invite you to lunch. We'll choose a quiet restaurant where we could talk.”

Noticing the undecided look of Hayri:

“I promise not to move the tables,” he said, with a funny laugh.

***

They chose a restaurant not too far from the hospital. Lunch time had already passed but the boss still gave them a good meal.

Hayri told him all of his memories of university years: his troubling relationship with Aysel, his future wife; his difficulties with courses; his problems with friends.

“I was left with one friend only: Rashad. He was always as weird as he used to be in high school. But we were getting along pretty well. I was apparently his only friend. All other students and residents of the dormitory were still trying to avoid him.”

“We sometimes went to the movies in town. On the bus, we were talking in French to keep our practice but also for others do not understand. He believed he was followed by some individuals.

Nadir raised his eyebrows.

“Yes, he thought he was followed,” said Hayri. Sometimes, walking in the streets of the city, we suddenly change our direction. He felt these diversions were necessary to shake off our pursuers. He always believed in telepathy. More than ever. One day he told me he had sex with a girl in the library. Not physically, but telepathically.”

Nadir interrupted:

“People with schizophrenia can take their hallucinations for telepathy.”

“Those years, I did not know much about schizophrenia. I did not know how much he was sick. I just thought he was a bit eccentric. Everything he told amused me. I was very proud to be his only friend. That particular year, his friendship was my only success. All went well with him, until...”

Nadir nodded as if he already knew the end.

“Once, on my return from a school activity, I saw a note taped to the door of my dormitory room. The director wanted to see everyone in the room. When I went to his office, the other occupants of the room were already there, except Rashad. The manager told us that our friend had gone mad and an ambulance had taken him to the hospital.”

Nadir did not fail to notice Hayri’s desolation.

“Did you visit him, at the hospital?”

“I tried but I was told that I could not see him for several weeks. Then I could make a short visit. He did not talk to me. We were in May and final exams were approaching. Unfortunately, I could not make a second visit. And after the exams, I went to Istanbul.

“Did you see him again?”

“Yes, I saw him one more time when he returned to college in early October, after the holidays. He told us that he was healed. But a schizophrenic never heals, does he? I felt he was not as friendly as before, with me. He was always followed by some individuals. He called them ‘they’. But the worst was when he told me: *I know! You're nothing but one of them!*”

“I was shocked! He wasn’t trusting me anymore. I was nothing but one of ‘them’. Whoever ‘them’ was. Probably one of the individuals who kept following him. The next day he was gone. One of my roommates told me that he had put all his stuff in his suitcase and left without even saying goodbye. Since then I have never seen him. I was proud to be the only one to win his confidence. He had been my only success in friendship. I was disappointed by my failure and his unexpected departure.”

Hayri paused. Nadir stayed silent to respect this time of sorrow for his patient. Finally he spoke:

“Despite his illness, Rashad should have exerted a great influence on you.”

Hayri had never thought about it, at least not this way. He stared into the eyes Nadir without knowing what to say. The doctor may be right.

He felt the vibration of the BlackBerry in his pocket.

“Excuse me for a moment, he said. I have to go to the bathroom.”

He walked to the back of the restaurant. Once out of sight, he took the phone from his pocket to see who had called. This was Esther. A satisfied smile relaxed his face.

He called back. After the usual greetings, Esther clarified she was driving to Besançon[80], in the company of colleagues.

"You're going to Besançon with colleagues?" asked Hayri, surprised.

She explained that she was traveling with two professors who had invited her to give a lecture and University of Besançon. She would spend the weekend in Franche-Comté[81], would visit the historic sites and Monday she would give her lecture in the auditorium of the University. Her return to Paris was scheduled for Wednesday.

She continued by inviting him to join her. Hayri could take the train tonight or early tomorrow morning.

"With the TGV[82], it lasts less than two hours. We can spend a few days together," she said.

Spending a few days with Esther was not a bad idea. But they had to cut the conversation short since she was the one who was driving,

"I would like to, but I have to organize myself. I'll call you back," he said, hanging up.

Could he really extend his 'vacation' for a couple of days? But no, it was not possible. He should start working soon. On the other hand, travelling to another city did not look like a good idea. When he returned to the table, he

[80] A city near the Swiss border.
[81] Administrational division of the region around Besançon.
[82] TGV: High speed train.

discovered that Nadir had already paid the bill. When leaving the restaurant the BlackBerry vibrated again. Hayri replied thinking it was still Esther.

Error! This was Sinan Bey.

“Mon cher, I've got news for you,” he said.

Damn! It was not the time.

“Sorry Sinan Bey, I'm in a meeting. May I call you later?” he said, hanging up quickly.

What he did was rude but he did not want to hear the incredible stories of ‘secret agents’.

Hayri and Nadir began to walk slowly back to the hospital.

“Shall we continue with hypnosis?” asked Nadir.

“Yes, said Hayri. This time, I am determined to go all the way down.”

Nadir stopped, which irritated Hayri. He could never stand people who kept stopping a walk, whenever they wanted to talk.

“Is this the desire to heal yourself or just the curiosity?” asked the doctor.

Ah, this man was a real psychologist. He was reading his mind.

“Both,” answered Hayri.

The BlackBerry made a short ‘beep’ when entering Nadir’s office. He had forgotten to turn it off. It was a message from Sinan Bey. Hayri hesitated. Would he take a look, or turn the phone off to read the message later? Naturally, curious like cats, he pressed the button and the message showed up on the screen:

The true identity of the man in the coma is discovered.

He had completely forgotten that there was a man in a coma. A man hit a few days ago by the car he was in.

He had no desire to return this call. He was tired of talking to Sinan Bey. He had to deal with its own problems, yet knowing that curiosity would devour him.

To drive the message off his head, he began to speak:

"What I saw as a dream, in the session before lunch, was like a video clip."

"I will add the price of the video clip to the bill," said Nadir, laughing.

Then he became serious.

"Think about it, he said. You should have seen a movie or heard a story like the one you told me during your hypnosis. Make an effort to remember it."

"I really do not remember anything like that, doctor. It was just a weird dream."

"Hayri, you're a symbolist. And Eurydice is only a symbol."

He watched the expression on Hayri's face few seconds before continuing:

"And remember, a 'look' was enough to make her disappear forever."

"Are you sure that Eurydice or the 'symbol' as you say, will disappear from my dreams?"

"It is up to you to discover. All she wants is to be seen. Once she knows she is seen, she will leave you alone."

"So, let's start," said Hayri.

He lay on his back. He accepted the red scarf handed by Nadir without objection and put it on his face.

Nadir put his hand on his forehead. He pulled it a few minutes later when they reached the hypnotic state.

Hayri began to speak in a trembling voice:

“I feel it! It is there, I feel someone’s breath on my neck!”

“Calm down Hayri. I am close to you. Try to turn your head slowly,” whispered Nadir, in his ear.

“I want to run away but I can’t. My feet are in lead shoes.”

Hayri’s body began to tremble like in a seizure. “I'm afraid!” he shouted with a terrified voice.

Nadir put his hand back on his forehead.

“Calm down Hayri. She means no harm to you. All you have to do is to turn your head back and look at her.”

“I can’t! I can’t!”

Nadir hesitated, should he stop the session or let Hayri push on through.

“Look behind you Hayri! Look behind!” he yelled, for the last time.

In his hypnotic dream, Hayri made a tremendous effort to obey this order. He felt a crack in his neck, but finally managed to turn his head.

And he looked back...

XI

Seven young men, in love with Mehlika Sultan,
Walked out at night by the gate of the city.

Yahya Kemal Beyatlı

You are nothing but one of them!

Stunned by the light sparkling from everywhere, I stopped. My legs are trembling with fatigue. I am breathless.

I raise my head to look at the sky flooded with sun light that blinds me at the moment. I close my eyes. I can't reopen them until after several attempts.

I look in all directions but don't see anything. There is nothing around, not even the 'thing'. By instinct, I look for a place to hide, just in case.

I am in the middle of a field, a vast fallow field. Far away to the horizon, I see mountains. There are no trees for as far as the eye can see. Some bushes draw the edges between fields. Everything seems sterile.

Astonished, I look all around, again and again. There is no living creature in sight. How did I end up here?

I remember I was recently with Nadir, in his office, lying on his 'dentist' chair, trying to dive into dreams, to get rid of the thing.

Ah, the 'thing!' But I do not see it! So I managed to make it disappear!

Satisfied with my victory, I smile.

Suddenly, I think I hear a voice. I look around panicked but see nothing.

A few seconds later, I hear it again. Clearer this time...

"Farid!"

I lower my head. I make myself little and try to identify where the voice is coming from.

At this point, I notice a dirt road to my right. A path, narrow path between the fields. A girl on the path waving.

Since there is no one else around, she must be waving for me. I still look in all directions to make sure I am alone.

She is dressed like a peasant. A blue skirt with rose petals and a yellow shirt. A white scarf partially hides her black hair. She shouts again:

"Farid!"

Despite a hundred meters between us, a light wind carries her voice to me. Is she lost in this rural area? I start walking towards her.

"Are you calling me?" I ask.

As I approach, the girl smiles. Like most peasants, she has white teeth. She is beautiful.

"Farid. What are you doing here? Everyone is looking for you," she says.

I return her smile.

"I am afraid I am not the one you're looking for."

"But I wish, I was," I tell myself.

Then I notice the piercing color of her green eyes. A green that I have never seen before.

"So, you prefer I call you by your nickname from Istanbul or Ankara?" she says wryly.

It is a voice that reveals her confidence and trust in herself. Her light makeup reveals that she is not a real peasant.

But that is not all. She is speaking French:

"Réveille-toi Farid! Tu n'es plus à Istanbul![83]"

"Do you speak French!?"

"Better than you," she replies, surprising me for the second time.

I feel stupid, I remain silent for a few seconds. Then I ask curiously:

"How do you know that I speak Fr... ?"

[83] Wake up, Farid! You are no longer in Istanbul.

She looks at me with her green eyes. I can't finish my phrase.

It is time that this hypnosis session ends. I pinch myself in various parts of my body to wake me up but it only serves to hurt me. Nadir! Why doesn't he intervene? Apparently, I'm stuck in this 'hypnotic dream.'

But maybe it would be better to continue. This girl is unlike any creature I have ever seen so far.

"I'm Hayri," I say with my best smile. The smile that I made for myself when I was sixteen, practicing in front of the mirror. It usually helped me to pick up girls.

"And I am Marie Antoinette, the queen of France," she says, with a laugh.

Is she making fun of me?

Finally she begins to walk away. A few steps later, she stops to look back at me.

"What are you waiting for? Everyone is worried about you. We need you come back!" she says.

"To come where?"

She starts to walk away without answering my question. An irresistible desire forces me to follow, like being pulled by a magnet.

"I know you're not sick," she says. "This is a story you made up to come back home, isn't it?"

She still takes me for someone else, but who?

"I'm not sick."

"I know, I just told you. But you should not do like that, Farid. You should finish your college education."

What is she talking about?

She takes me by hand. At her touch, I feel a slight dizziness. This girl is really irresistible. My god! Please make this dream never end!

I don't dare asking her name. She probably thinks I already know it. After ten minutes of walk through the empty fields, suddenly, houses appear at the end of the path.

We finally arrive at a small square surrounded by a few houses. They are all made of earth. A group of people huddled among the houses are looking at us.

"Here they are!" shouts one of the women at our approach.

We are in a small village. It looks like one of the villages of Eastern Anatolia or the Middle East, where terrorists continue to play djirit[84]. Everything is like in pictures that one can often see in the news on TV.

A young man approaches and yells at me:

"Where were you? Your mother is sick, because of you!"

He scares me. Luckily an old man pulls his arm.

"Calm down, Ahmet," he says. "You know that your friend is sick."

Then he tells me in an angry tone:

"Go to see your mother at home, Farid."

[84] Djirit or Jirit: Old, traditional Turkish game. In figurative sense: Doing whatever you want, without control.

But this is crazy. Who are these people? Why do they all call me 'Farid'?

"I'm not Farid!" I say aloud.

They all shake heads, looking at me with pity.

"Come," says my companion.

She takes me by the hand and brings me into a house.

Once inside, I can't see anything because of the contrast in brightness with the outside. Blinded, I let myself guided by the girl who apparently knows the inside of the house.

I hear a suffering voice:

"Is that you, Mehlika?"

"Yes mom," says the girl and she guides me to the wooden stairs.

So, her name is 'Mehlika!'

But she said 'mom.' Are we brother and sister?

This dream could turn into a nightmare. I pinch my arm hard, it still does not wake me up.

"Nadir, please wake me up!" I say, aloud.

The girl throws me an angry look. I see that these beautiful soft eyes can easily change expression.

"Stop acting!" she says softly.

"Did you find Farid?" says the voice from upstairs.

"Yes mom. He's with me."

Suddenly, I understand. These people need some 'Farid', who may even not exist at all, and they bring me here to the role of substitute?

They must be all crazy.

However, I do not worry too much. After all, it is only a dream. Even if it turns into a nightmare, it will have an end, right? Nadir, my cell phone or alarm clock will pull me from this slumber. I just have to wait and continue to play this comedy that takes a rather an absurd turn.

***

Two weeks later, I lost all hope. Nadir had forgotten me. He was either asleep or worse, dead.

Or, he left me in a state of hypnosis on the incline chair, under the red scarf and walked out to wander in the streets of Paris. Is he hit by a car?

Will someone come and get me? The maid, the night guard with his dog?

Maybe the time flows at a different speed in a dream than in the real world. Maybe half an hour is equivalent to a week in a dream?

I had the biggest shock when I finally looked in the mirror. This was not me! The mirror was reflecting the image of another person. A person I knew some time ago: that of Rashad!

Rashad and Farid, are they one and same person?

I was trapped in a body that was not mine. Younger, but not mine. For a moment, I had lost control and broke the mirror. An act that I regretted immediately. Mehlika was very frightened because the old lady, our so called 'mother' had a heart attack.

Every day, her illness was getting worse and in this forgotten corner of the world, there was not a single doctor. The tears that I saw in those beautiful green eyes were making me sad.

Since the death of my father, my 'real' father, I was angry with God. I still tried to say a few prayers that I had learned in elementary school, without really knowing what to beg for.

A weeks later, I finally confessed myself that I was desperately in love with this girl who was supposed to be my sister.

She told me about her life, 'our' life, believing that I had forgotten everything because of a mental illness. Our father, who died ten years ago, had sent both of us to Istanbul. She had studied at the school of the sisters, which explained how she learned French. Her father, 'our' father, who had seen how the future would be, had tried to keep his children away from danger.

***

One day a neighbor, Hassan, offered me to accompany him on his motorcycle to town. I accepted because I could buy some medicine for the old woman. In addition, a little change would do me good.

The roads were rendered dangerous by the activists of the guerrilla patrolling everywhere. Nevertheless, we managed to reach the city without incident.

I immediately realized how much I missed the city. Hassan and I decided to separate, to join later. I walked into the first pharmacy. While the pharmacist was preparing the medicines, I consulted a calendar hanging on the wall. It was from the year 1998.

“Do you have a new calendar?” I asked to the pharmacist.

“But we are in 1998,” he said.

He looked at me with suspicion. He must have thought I was crazy.

So we were in 1998! The year I was in still in college. So, is there a ‘Hayri’ in Ankara?

It was like swimming in the mystery. All of a sudden, an idea came to my mind. A crazy one.

“Do you have a phone?”

“Yes, come here,” said an old man sitting behind the counter.

I dialed the number. My heart began to beat loudly when I heard the bell ringing at the other end of the wire. After a few seconds that seemed interminable to me, I heard the 'click' of unhook.

“Hello?”

Recognizing the voice of my mother, my heart started to beat like crazy.

“Hello?” she said again.

“Mom it’s me, Hayri.” I said finally.

“Hayri?” How are you, my son?

What was I supposed to tell her?

“I'm fine, Mom.”

“And your exams? Are you doing well?”

She was thinking I was still in Ankara, at the university. We were in the 1998!.

“Everything is well mom. I am getting good grades. All A and B.”

I was lying. My grades were terrible that year.

“And Aysel, how is she? Are you getting alone well?”

There is a girl in my life: Aysel, the beautiful girl who would become my wife later. She is still alive.

“Of course, Mom.”

But this is not correct. Why am I lying in a hypnotic-dream?

“Mom. I have something important to tell you.”

How to explain all this? My hypnosis, my dream, my travel in time, my new address and especially my new body?

“What is that important thing, my son?”

The sudden change in her voice was reflecting her concern. Like all mothers, she was worried for her only son.

“I love you, mom.”

“I love you too, my son. Are you coming to Istanbul for the Feast of Ramadan?”

“I do not know yet. I must prepare for my exams coming right after the Feast.

“Good luck, my son,” she says.

“Thank you mom. Goodbye.”

“Goodbye my son.”

Hanging up, I got a chill. I just had made a conversation with a world that existed several years ago.

* * *

On my way back with Hassan, I made the decision to end this nonsense. I no longer want to live in fiction, in a different time and especially in a different body belonging to someone else.

After giving her the medicine, I would say “goodbye Mehlika” and I would leave for Istanbul. Yes, I was in love with this girl, but I could no longer continue the life of a voluntary prisoner.

After all, she loves me like a brother. Even if she has hidden feelings, they would only be for Farid, not for me. Especially not for Hayri, she had not even seen.

I would lower my look to avoid the power of wet green eyes and tell her: “I have to go, Mehlika. I will come back to pick you up, in a few years.”

I would abandon her there with her mother and I would flee, like a coward!

Ah! If I could take her with me.

My thoughts were interrupted when Hassan stopped the motorcycle.

“Why are we stopping?” I ask.

“Look over there,” he says, in a trembling voice.

At about fifties meters ahead on the road, there were four men. The setting sun was stretching their shadows up to us. They were armed with Kalashnikovs.

Instinctively, I looked back. There were two more. We were surrounded.

They approached slowly from both sides talking and laughing among themselves, as if they were not interested in us.

Finally one of them spoke to us:

"Chevbach[85] Hassan. Chevbach Farid."

Surprise! But they know my name.

"They are terrorists," said Hassan.

Although he spoke in whispers, they heard. The biggest guy in the group yelled:

"You should be ashamed to treat us as 'terrorists', my brother!"

He pushed Hassan who fell to the ground.

"You have no shame?" repeated the other.

They gave him a kick. Poor Hassan, tried in vain to protect himself with his hands. Within seconds, his face flooded with blood.

"Come on!" said one of the men with Kalashnikovs.

He pulled me by the arm. I obeyed. We began climbing the hill near the road. The others stayed behind and continued to beat Hassan.

They were out of sight when I suddenly heard Hassan screaming:

"You are terrorists! That's what you are! You..."

His words were cut off by the neat snap of the Kalashnikov.

---

[85] Good evening (Kurdish)

I was horrified. My escort tried to calm me down.

“Don’t worry, he said, with a bitter smile. There is no danger to you. You are privileged.”

I did not dare asking “why?”

We walked for over an hour without speaking. He wasn’t treating me like a prisoner. However, I did not dare asking where we were going.

We finally arrived at a sort of camp composed of camouflage tents. On adjacent land, a dozen men were training with military equipment.

I was in the middle of these people and was not supposed to use the word ‘terrorist’ which was striking their susceptibility violently.

My guide made me stop in front of a tent larger than the others.

“Wait here,” he said and entered the tent alone.

I began to look around. There was not much to see. Near the tent, a large satellite dish drew my attention.

Several questions swarmed in my head: Why did they bring me here? Are they going to shoot me too? If not, what do they want from me? Why was I privileged? Who was I to these people?

Suddenly, an idea sparked in my brain. After all, this was nothing but a dream. Or rather hallucinations caused by this stupid hypnosis that lasted a little too long. On the other hand if they kill me, shall I not end up waking up in the office of Nadir, in Paris?

Unless I am really schizophrenic.

Everything that is going on around me, would therefore be nothing but the fruit of my own hallucinations. Maybe I have a split personality. All because of this stupid hypnosis. I should stay away from psychologists. They make you sicker than you are.

I started reviewing what to do: I could run towards this group of individuals who played the soldiers in the training ground and shout: “You are terrorists! You are terrorists!”

A dozen of Kalashnikovs would turn on me. I would hear their “taca, taca, taca!” Then everything would be over.

I smiled in spite of myself. I would never have the courage to do such a thing. In addition, there was no guarantee that I would wake up in the office of Nadir in Paris. Instead, I could find myself in the middle of a crowd of dead people walking to hell.

I pinched myself. It hurt me bad, but still did not woke me.

“Nadir!” I said, blowing through my teeth: “Wake me up, please!”

“Are you're talking to yourself, my friend?”

My guide had just walked out of the tent. He was looking at me with an amused smile. By raising the curtain-door he invited me to enter. It was weird, he was treating me as a guest.

The brightness of the sun outside, prevented me from seeing anything inside until my eyes adjusted.

There was a table in the middle of the tent, nothing else. A person sitting on a chair, was typing something on a laptop.

I was surprised when my escort introduced me in English:

"Jane, Farid is here."

This was a woman dressed as a man in fatigues, who was she? Where was I? She stopped typing and looked at me over her glasses then spoke:

"Do you speak English?"

"Are you American?" I said, surprised.

She made sign to my guide to walk out, then spoke looking straight into my eyes:

"My nationality has no importance, neither yours. In this place, those are not our passports that characterize us."

Her eyes went back to the computer screen. She tapped something. She was surely communicating via the satellite antenna mounted outside of the tent. After a few transactions, it appeared to have received sufficient information. Her blonde hair was contrasting with everything else of this country.

She handed me a paper.

"Read it to me."

It was a cutout from a French newspaper, Le Figaro or France-Soir, an article about soccer.

"Aloud," she said.

Who does she think she is? Noticing my irritation on the face, she changed her tone.

"S'il vous plait[86]," she said in French, with a strong American accent.

I reluctantly obeyed her will and began to read. She stopped me after a few lines.

"This is good. You have a natural French accent."

So what? Is this a job interview?

"Adar, come here!" she shouted.

My guide showed his head through the curtain. So, his name was Adar.

"Take him to the commander," she said.

She stooped smiling and went back to the computer screen. The blood rushed to my head.

"Who are you and why are you keeping me here?" I said angrily.

The shock was big. She looked at me for a moment as if I was an insolent boy. Then she smiled again, indulgently.

"I think I've already mentioned here, our nationalities and identities are irrelevant. We brought you here for a special mission. You will have the details as your training progress."

"My training?" I asked, with surprise.

"Don't worry. The mission will be easy. As I said earlier, we are going to explain everything when the time comes."

"And what if I do not want to do this 'mission' you mention?"

"But of course you want. We do not want any harm to your sister, do we?"

---

[86] Please

Ah! That's it! Here is their weapon: the blackmail; more powerful than the Kalashnikovs.

Speaking of 'my sister' I suddenly remembered the contents of my pocket.

"I brought medicine for her .., my mother. It should...."

"It won't be necessary, she said dryly. Your mother died this morning, just after you left for the city."

I felt sorry, especially for Mehlika.

"My condolences," she said slowly.

I rushed out of the tent. Adar followed me.

"I'm sorry for your loss," he said. "Tomorrow, I'll take you to the village for burial ceremony."

God thank! I will see Mehlika again. Maybe for the last time.

"Adar!" she called from inside.

Adar told me to wait and entered back in the tent.

I could hear their conversation but since they were talking in a low voice, I did not understand all the words. I still clearly distinguished few of them: "University, interrupted studies, schizophrenia..."

Obviously, they were talking about me. Who else could they talk about? Do they really think I am schizophrenic? ...

A few minutes later, Adar came and threw me a look of pity. Although it seemed unbearable, it might be the game that I should play.

And if they were right? As a prisoner in the body of Farid, I could also be affected by this disease. Maybe all these: the hypnosis, the terrorist camp, the blonde woman, were nothing but the spectra of my hallucinations.

And Mehlika? Is she an illusion too?

***

During the funeral, rather modest, I have been acting like a real brother to Mehlika. She wept, resting her head on my shoulder. I got lost in the greenness of her wet eyes.

She had her mother's eyes. But why mine, or rather those of Farid were brown?

Adar explained the reason on our way back to camp.

“Because of your illness, you must have forgotten certain things. Try to remember. Mehlika’s mother is the second wife of your father. Mehlika came to your home with her mother. You two have no blood ties. Do you remember when we were kids, you told me that you will marry her when you grow up?”

These words paralyzed me. He noticed that I was shocked. To seduce Mehlika, I had Farid as rival, whose body had captured me. A body with a sick head.

It was the perfect time to extract some information from Adar.

“You and me, we were friends?”

Adar had the same look of pity. He made me sit on a rock. For a couple of minutes, without saying a word, we looked at the valley spread out at our feet.

“It's a pity that you do not remember of our childhood dreams,” he said.

He gave me a little slap on the cheek as a sign of friendship.

"Remember. With Mehlika and Dilan, we would run from this country.”

“And where would we go?” I asked.

His answer surprised me once again:

“But in America, dammit!”

This ‘terrorist’ who glanced thoughtfully the valley, was still a child.

“So why not do it now?” I asked with hope. “We can return to the village, take Mehlika and Dilan, and...”

He put his hand over my mouth to shut me up.

“Are you crazy?” he said. “Even if we manage to escape, the Organization will find us and kill us.”

“But why? The woman in the tent, is she not an American?”

“You studied at the school of priests in Istanbul. You even went to university and graduated with some degree but you are still naive, my friend!” he said, in an angry tone.

What was he talking about? He surely knew things I didn’t.

“We are murderers! They are searching for us everywhere. There is not a single country in this world that would accept us as ordinary immigrants.”

As Hayri, I did not kill anyone. But Farid?

"You do not remember, do you?" he asked.

"Remember what?"

"You and I, when we were fifteen years old. You had come from Istanbul for the summer holidays. The Organization had recruited us temporarily for 'training'. After having learned how to use a Kalashnikov, they had put us in a battalion. We have been watching the road leading to the city. Don't you remember?"

In response, I just looked at him stupidly. He continued his story:

"We stopped a bus that was going to Ankara. There was a group of engineers who were returning from a visit to the factory in the region, all dressed in ties. You still don't remember?

"No," I said.

He looked at me with patience. He was trying to figure out if I was honest with the failure of my memory or making fun of him.

"Our commander told us to remove only men who wore ties, but not bother other travelers in the bus. We lead the engineers off and let the bus go. Once it was out of sight, we made our way to the mountains with the prisoners."

He paused for a few seconds. I felt he needed to put his memories in order. The rest of the story seemed frightening.

"One of the detainees had understood what would happen to them. You and me, we saw him discreetly removing his tie and putting in pocket. Then, he began to whine and beg us not to kill him. The commander came to see, and when he noticed that he had no tie, he yelled at us."

Adar looked at me, curious to know if I remembered at least the end of the story.

"You, told the commander that it was your mistake and you asked forgiveness. The commander had left the man go. He was saved by his trick."

"What happened then?"

"They were twelve engineers. You and I, we took them behind a rock and shot."

I jumped.

"You and me? Why only us, and not the others? And the commander, where was he?"

"But it is the custom, said Adar. Novices, as we were, always begin their training by killing someone. This way you lose your 'virginity' and you become a true fighter.

"I don't think I would be able to kill anyone!" I said, terrified.

Amar smiled bitterly:

"Yes you can. You've done it several times."

***

My training began the next day. I was surprised by my dexterity. I was hitting the center of the target, effortlessly. Kalashnikov became an instrument that I could not stay away from. I had never felt myself so powerful. Jane was giving me some pills that I swallowing twice a day. Those pills were helping me to heal. At least this is what they were telling me.

In fact, I didn't care much of what was said to me but I obeyed their instructions. Because they allowed me to go and see Mehlika twice a week.

Besides Jane, there was another woman in the camp. Her name was Dilan. She was sleeping with the commander. Adar was saddening every time he saw her.

One night towards the end of the third week of my training, I was told to go see Jane in her tent. I had just returned from the village. I was happy to have spent the whole day with Mehlika.

Jane received me with a smile. That was unusual. There were two men in the tent that I was seeing for the first time. They spoke English with a strange accent. Their physical appearance hinted they were from a Nordic country.

On the desk of Jane, there was an open box. Packing peanuts were scattered all around. As I approached, one of the men pulled out an object wrapped in plastic bubble sheets. Jane spoke to him in a language that was completely unknown to me. How many languages was this women speaking?

They opened the package carefully. There was a metal pipe of about 30 inches in length and as thick as my arm.

"This is M72," the man said in English.

Jane's eyes turned to me:

"Did you already use it?"

"No, I said. What the hell is this?"

All three laughed.

"These gentlemen will train you. And in a few weeks, you are going to be an expert," said Jane.

The word 'gentleman' echoed in my brain for the next couple of hours.

***

A few months later, I was in Beirut with Mehlika. Without her, I would never have done this trip. In fact, it was them who had suggested that she joins me. They told:

"Couples are more likely to go undetected."

In Beirut, the traces of the civil war were more or less erased. The Organization had rented an apartment in the Christian Quarter of the city.

We were happy. Mehlika found a job of selling tickets at an airline company and I started to work for a company that was selling generators. There were frequent power cuts and luxurious buildings in the city needed electricity.

I was surprised when Mehlika told me she was born in Beirut. She even tried to test my knowledge of French by asking "How do you call the people of Beirut?" I knew the answer thank to a Lebanese restaurant where I dined during a trip to Europe: *La Beyrouthine.*

Mehlika, who was an optimistic in nature, sent a letter to the United States to participate in the Green Card Lottery. "You never know," she said.

She had no idea what we were here for. As for me, I had almost forgotten that I was living all this in a hypnotic-dream. A dream that I did not want to wake up. I could spend the rest of my life like that, with Mehlika, if the Organization left us alone. I was praying that they forget us.

One day, a phone call made us understand that they had not forgotten...

***

A new training began for me. Monday, a driver with a car met me very early in the morning in front of the Holiday Inn. After a three-hour trip, we passed the border and arrived at an abandoned village.

The M72 LAW was an anti-tank rocket launcher, not a child's toy. I started to practice on the abandoned armored tanks of Saddam dating from the Gulf War. There was another person with me. A slightly older man. He had a sinister look. We were always together but never exchanged more than a couple of words. Not only because our guards did not allow us but also because we did not want to. I guessed he was also schizophrenic. A more advanced case.

Every day we followed specific scenarios. We hid behind the bushes and we made surprise attacks against the dead metal vehicles, turning them into Swiss cheese with our M72s. I had no idea what we were trained for, and I did not care.

I returned Thursday before sunset, to find myself in the arms of Mehlika. We stayed in the house during the weekend, and we hated Mondays like everyone. Despite opposition from Mehlika, I regularly took drugs they were giving me. I was happy than ever, powerful and capable of anything.

This program continued a couple of weeks. One day we had visitors, a man and a woman. They told me that my exercises were completed. I was ready for the mission and I was going on a trip. Mehlika would come with me, thus eliminating any objections from my side. They took our photos and left.

They returned another night to bring us two passports. We were now two French citizens, Evelyn and Bernard. We were not married but we would play the role of a young French couple.

I thought they were going to tell me what would my 'mission' be but they said they knew nothing about it either. However, they assured us that after the mission, we would return to Beirut and they would leave us alone.

They also gave us two tickets. I was surprised to see that our destination was Cyprus. There, we would receive the rest of us our instructions. We would have the privilege of staying at the Golden Tulip Hotel. After all, we were just tourists.

***

During approach to Larnaca Airport, I asked Mehlika to pass my pills. I wanted to swallow them before landing. She checked in vain in her bag but could not find them.

Arriving at the hotel, I searched the suitcase. There was no trace of my medication. I became furious. I saw the panic in the green eyes of Mehlika but I could not control myself.

I went down to the lobby to talk to the receptionist. I ended up by yelling her. Suddenly, I felt someone touching my shoulder. It was the security guard of the hotel. He was holding my pills in his hand.

"Your girlfriend has found them," he said, with a polite smile.

Back into the room, I found Mehlika in tears.

"Forgive me," she said. "I do not trust people who sent us here. I thought they gave these pills to drug you. I did not know that you can't do without them!"

She was right. There was something fishy in this case. But what?

"Put your bathing suit on," I told. "Let us swim in the warm Mediterranean Sea."

Lying on the sand, I tried to think clearly. I should find a way to save us before I drove Mehlika into this trap.

When I was taking my medication, I could not think clearly but I was calm and obedient. On the other hand, if I did not take them, I was turning into a suffering monster. This had already happened a few times during our stay in Beirut but never as strong as the day of our arrival at the hotel in Larnaca.

Ideas were like swarming bees in my head. We were in southern Cyprus. The northern part of the island was controlled by the Turkish community; so called Turkish Republic of Northern Cyprus. We could flee there. And from there, we could go in Turkey.

For a few days, I was haunted by this idea that seemed crazy and dangerous. The Greek Cypriot soldiers could shoot us. Even if we manage to cross the border, this time the Turkish Cypriots could kill us, even before explaining who we are.

And really, who were we?

I asked the receptionist that I yelled at the first day for some sleeping pills. She procured without questioning. The management did not want any problems with customers. Sleeping pills made me sleep like a baby. I remembered that Hayri also was taken them.

Hey! I think of him as another person. But Hayri is me, isn't he?

Another idea came to mind. This period of my life that I lived in the body of someone else, was terrible.

The date I was launched hypnotically in Rashad's past life, rather Farid's, was approaching! And when that day would come, what was going to happen? Would I just wake up in a Nadir's inclined chair?

All these thoughts gave me headaches. It was hard to be a schizophrenic.

***

The Air France flight Larnaca - Paris was full of tourists. They were shouting, laughing, and having fun.

Mehlika's head was on my shoulder. She had fallen asleep shortly after the takeoff. Her hand resting on my knee had the ring that I had bought in Beirut.

I smiled. Ten days had passed since we had met a Hodja[87] in the Muslims quarter of Beirut. Everything was easy with Muslims. The Hodja, had made us first repeat some verses in Arabic to ensure that we are Muslims. He had not considered it necessary to check if I was circumcised or not. I wasn't sure if I had the right of having that operation in this body that was not mine.

---

[87] Hodja: Muslim priest

Then, the Hodja had married us with a ceremony of five minutes. How convenient it was.

“What would you like to drink, monsieur?”

The hostess had brought us meals. I had to refuse so as not to disturb ‘my wife’. At the hotel, we had a great breakfast on the balcony of our room, watching the sunrise.

Despite the sedative effect of the drugs and the loud chatter of passengers, I was trying to think.

Our honeymoon was over. “To work!” had said the voice on the phone. But what do they want me to do for them? What is that mission that I am trained for?

The idea that they would leave us alone after the mission was my only consolation. But ‘they’ would never leave us alone, would they? There would be more missions, one after another.

I looked out the window. The sky was cloudless. We were over the Mediterranean see. There was too much light, I lowered the curtain.

Once in Paris, we might be able to take refuge in the Turkish Embassy.

But what I can say at the Embassy? Wasn’t Turkey a country already invaded by legal and illegal immigrants coming from Iran, Syria and Iraq?

It was even possible to see the Africans, the ‘niggers’, trying to sell anything in the streets of Istanbul. Poor guys, as they had no other choice, they were all becoming peddlers for the local mafia.

So why Turkey would accept us?

I put my hand on the hand of Mehlika and closed my eyes.

***

And finally, this is the D day.

Sitting at a table in a café with a cup of chocolate, I try to see the other side of the river. The rain had stopped and the sun was sending its honey rays over the sky of Paris.

'Honey rays.' Those are not my words. I should have read or heard it somewhere, maybe in a book, long time ago, when I was a kid.

This is weird. I am about to do something horrible and I become romantic.

The alarm of a car starts screaming. This is the first signal. I know there are people waiting like me, hiding somewhere. In principle, I do not know them. I do not know from where they are watching the scene. But I can still notice one of them. This man who pretend looking the drawings of a bookseller, I recognize him. This is the other schizophrenic who received the same training as me: the M72. His backpack looks heavy. It is not difficult to guess what is in it.

I count up to twenty and I get up. I walk to the toilet. On the door of one of the cabins, there is a sign: *Closed for repair*.

I force the door that seems stuck and I enter. I put my feet on the seat to get to the height of a grid on the wall, near the ceiling. I easily remove the grid and take the bag waiting there for me. Then I return to my table and take a big gulp of chocolate that burns my tongue.

Last night, the voice at phone had told me these words:

"It is going to be an armored car. It does not have a diplomatic plate but an ordinary Parisian registration. Do not freak out. Wait until the car reaches the middle of the bridge. Then you do your job."

According to the plan, me and the guy who waits outside the bookseller, are going to attack first. Once the doors are open, by the impact of our shots, we will disappear. Then a third guy will come on the scene with his gun to finish the task with the passenger sitting in the back seat, if she is not already dead.

The second signal startles me. It is always the same annoying car alarm.

My heart starts beating wildly. I am not sure I want to do this. But this is not the time to fail. I take another sip of my chocolate as if it is necessary. I see that the guy of the bookseller who begins to walk towards the bridge. I get up. I must hurry!

Then I hear a beep sound. This one is weird, like a buzzing in the ears. My legs begin to shake. Am I going to faint?

I take a few steps. I feel a heavy weight on my shoulders, I can't hear anything other than this 'beep' which is coming from nowhere.

"My god," I say. "Help me!"

Funny! I pray to God I do not believe.

Despite my disbelief, God helps. All of a sudden, I see everything.

But I do know the 'target' of our mission. The person we are going to kill is not the consul, but Hayri! In other words it is 'me!'

I begin to run wildly. On my way, I push the guy of the bookseller. He falls to the ground. I don't know where the other assassin is. I have to run fast and stop the car before it reaches the bridge.

Arrived in the middle of the bridge, I stop and I throw my load into the river. Damn! There is a barge passing. But the bag disappears in the sand it carries.

I get to the other side of the bridge. I can see the car approaching! Hayri, that is to say 'I', am inside!

But the car is speeding! It must be stopped!

The rain made the street slippery. I make a sign to stop the car. But my foot slips. The car strikes me at full speed.

My face hits the windshield. I see for a moment the eyes of the passenger sitting in the back seat. I am like looking in a mirror.

This is weird. I do not feel any pain. But slowly everything plunges into darkness. I hear a car alarm. I hear the sirens of police and ambulance. All fading slowly…

But what is that 'beep' sound that continues to buzz constantly in my ears?

XII

"The Gate of Hell will be closed to you!" said the old woman.
"Why?" asked Hayri, surprised.
"Your daughter was only five years old. The Day of Judgment, the children who died before the age of puberty, will be waiting at the Gate of the Hell; to prevent their parents from entering.[88]"

A walk in the sky

Something was blocking his vision. "This must be the red veil of Nadir," he thought. He took it off his eyes and put himself in sitting position.

Nadir was facing him.

"This is a funny story that you just told me," he said, with a grin.

[88] From a Muslim belief

Hayri, with a haggard look, carefully examined the room. He was indeed where his journey had begun. He was back, finally!

“I believe you won’t have nightmare anymore. You finally managed to disappear this ‘thing’ off your dreams. Congratulations!” said Nadir.

But the victory was his. Nadir was the hero of this healing.

Hayri put his feet on the ground and stood up. He did not move for a few moments. Then walked to the door.

“Are you leaving already?” asked Nadir.

Hayri did not seem to hear him. Like a robot, he opened the door and went out. Nadir, worried by the behavior of his patient, followed.

Once in the hallway, Hayri quickened his steps. He stopped for a few seconds in front of the elevator but did not have any patience to wait. He walked to the stairs and began to descend.

Arrived at the third, he rushed to the skywalk. The sliding door opened automatically. Upon entering the glass tunnel illuminated by the rays of the sun, he stopped.

His hesitation delayed him just a few seconds. He rushed again. Two nurses coming from the other side had to step aside to avoid a collision.

In less than a minute, he was in front of room 234. The chair of the guard was empty. He entered immediately.

The curtains were drawn, the room was dark. Only the continuous ‘beep’ sound coming from the electrocardiogram could be heard. The straight line on the screen was indicating a cardiac arrest.

“Doctor! Quick!” exclaimed a female voice sobbing.

He knew that voice. He approached the bed to look at the dead face of his friend Rashad, or rather Farid. Then his eyes turned to the woman he recognized immediately. His heart began to beat wildly.

A doctor and nurses rushed into the room.

“Please leave the room!” said one of them, with an authoritative voice.

“We will do all what is necessary,” said another.

“All what is necessary,” repeated Hayri between his teeth. There was no need to be a doctor to know that the patient was already dead.

He approached Mehlika, hold her by the arm and spoke softly:

“We must go out. Let’s leave them alone so they can do their job.”

She obeyed without resistance. They left together and walked away down the hall.

Hayri did not want to hear the sounds of electric shocks. It was as if a part of his own life that was dying in this room.

A few minutes later, one of the nurses left the room and approached.

“I'm sorry. My condolences,” she said, handing the wedding ring of Farid to Mehlika.

She collapsed in tears. They needed to move away from the scene. Hayri took her out, to the garden of the hospital.

It was cool. The pale sun hanging on the sky, part of the decor, was not warming. Hayri took his jacket and put it on the back of the young woman.

An empty bench was waiting for them. What can a man do better, other than offering his shoulder to console a woman? After shedding tears for a few minutes, Mehlika finally calmed.

She asked:

“Are you one of his friends?”

“We were old friends.”

He wanted to tell her everything. He wanted to say:

“Mehlika, don’t you recognize me? This is me Rashad, Farid or Hayri... I am the same man who loved you. Remember, you also loved me when I was in the body of Farid? It was me who bought you that ring at your finger, it was me you had love for the first time, it was me you gave your virginity, it was on my shoulder you cried during the funeral of your mother. I brought you from the past. I pulled you out from the dark universe and took to the surface of the earth. Orpheus could not save Eurydice but I did it.”

Fortunately, before he said all this nonsense, Sinan Bey joined them.

“My condolences madam,” he said, stooping cordially to shake hands with Mehlika.

***

Explanations of Sinan Bey

After driving Mehlika to her home, Sinan Bey took Hayri at the Embassy, at the Ankara Street.

“I have interesting things to say,” he said.

He took him into his office, made him sit in a chair in front of a monitor and began to speak:

"While citizens of western Turkey lived and still live like in paradise, eastern Turkey has always been a hell. For several decades the Organization recruited and trained the boys and girls to make them terrorists. Families worried for their children, have always been looking ways to save them. That's what happened to Farid and Mehlika. They were first sent by their father to study at foreign schools in Istanbul. You first met him in Diyarbakir then at the School of Brothers in Istanbul. This was a pseudo-name he used hoping to cover his track for his pursuers. Did he ever tell you about her sister who went to School of Sisters at the same time as you?"

Hayri preferred to leave this question unanswered.

"After the early death of their father, they had to return to their village. A few years later, Farid passed final examinations in secondary education in a local high school and went to Ankara for university studies."

"I know, said Hayri. I even shared my room with him in the dormitory."

"He had plans. After college, he wanted to go to the U.S. and live there. I think he had connections in this country. We also knew that his grand-grandmother was a survivor of Tehcir[89]."

"Tehcir?" asked Hayri, with a weird look.

Sinan Bey pretended not to notice his attitude.

[89] The Tehcir (Law): a temporary law passed by the Ottoman Parliament in 1915 authorizing the deportation of the Armenian population.

"He was schizophrenic and his illness was getting worse. He could no longer live among normal people. He had to return to his village. But this time, he has been recruited by the Organization to be formed as an international terrorist."

"An international terrorist?"

"Yes. Like you, he had learned French at High School and English in Prep. School at the university." said Sinan Bey.

"Should you be multilingual to become an international terrorist?"

"It is a necessary condition. He also has received training in several other areas, including using a LAW."

"LAW?" said Hayri faking a surprise.

"M72; 'Light Anti-armor Weapon' or LAW. A perfect weapon for such attacks. It can be used against the armored cars of presidents, prime ministers, ambassadors etc. It is not difficult to program a paranoid schizophrenic like Farid to do such a mission. French Anti-Terrorism Department had warned us of a possible attack against one of our diplomats; to the ambassador, or one of the consuls in mission in Paris. Since September 11, they changed their attitude and they decided to help us. They have realized that terror can hit them too."

"Do you mean the accident was not a real accident but an assassination attempt?"

"For some reason that we do not know, Farid changed his mind just before attacking the car you were in by coincidence. The driver was ordered to return to the embassy without taking the madam consul. This is a tactic we often use to cover their tracks. But you, poor fool! What did you do? You were drunk and you have accepted the invitation of Ahmet the driver. You have got into the car. You should know however that it is against the regulations.

"Why did he change his mind?" asked Hayri, as if he did not know the reason.

"We do not know yet. Maybe we will learn later. In my opinion, the Organization does not know more than us. You were not their true target, but after the accident, they followed you to understand what was going on."

Nobody will never know the real reason, thought Hayri. Then he asked curiously:

"And the woman with green eyes?"

"We are convinced that she knew nothing of the activities of her fiancé. She can even be totally innocent."

Hayri relieved hearing the word 'innocent'. Sinan Bey noticed the change of expression on the face of his friend.

"Ah, mon cher," he said, with a mischievous smile. "You still love chasing dangerous women!"

***

In accordance with the wishes of Mehlika, they buried Farid in the Muslim cemetery in Bobigny[90]. There were more people than Hayri had imagined. They all came to pay their respects to this 'unknown' deceased. Who could they be, all these people?

[90] Bobigny: a town in the northeastern suburbs of Paris.

On his way back, Hayri accompanied Mehlika to her home by taxi.

“I would like to invite you for a coffee but it is a mess in my apartment,” she said, descending.

“Another time, perhaps?” asked Hayri with his best smile.

With patience, he could possibly win back the heart of the woman he loved.

The ‘best smile’ had its effect.

“Would you like to come tomorrow, late in the afternoon?” she asked. Since you and Farid were old acquaintances both, I want to show you some of his belongings. I will also prepare Yalanci dolma[91]. We could have diner together, if you want.”

“Oh! Yes, with pleasure!” said Hayri.

She kissed him on the cheek.

“Thank you for coming to the funeral. I’ll see you tomorrow,” she said, getting of the taxi.

“See you tomorrow.”

It was a fun to reconquer a woman he already had conquered. He congratulated himself for his gift of seduction.

***

The last session

“How many times should I tell you? Hypnosis is not a sleep. This is only a state of ...”

[91] Yalanci dolma(a dish): rice-stuffed grape leaves

"Yes, yes, I understand," said Hayri impatiently. "But I just want to know why you did not take me out of the hypnotic state, despite my desperate calls for help. I asked for your help on several occasions. Why did you not wake me up? Did you not hear my calls for help?"

"I heard them all. But I was quite decided not to interrupt because I wanted you to go all the way to the end."

Hayri admitted that he had gone all the way to the end.

"So I will no more have nightmare when I sleep?" he asked.

"Never again. At least for this reason."

"So, all what I saw during my hypnosis sessions were telepathic messages sent by Farid? He told me the story of the last couple of years of his own life, as I was experiencing like my own?"

"Imagine that your friend in a coma emitted primitive messages with electromagnetic waves, like any brain is capable of doing. Your brain, receiving them, may have created its own images or 'video clips', as you said yourself." said Nadir

"But a man in a coma, can he send telepathic messages?"

"Hayri, for most scientists, telepathy does not exist, others are very skeptical. In addition, patients with schizophrenia may take their hallucinations as telepathic messages."

"But then!? What do you mean? Are we talking about telepathy or something else?"

"Many people do not believe in telepathy. However, several scientific studies have been launched by some companies who have already developed mobile telephones. In twenty years, we may be able to communicate without using any of the mobile phone devices that we are using today."

Was he serious? He was speaking like most of the science fiction fans who never had technical training.

"They will even charge us and we will have to pay for our telepathic messages," said Nadir with a laugh.

This time he was joking.

Hayri was still suspicious about all this. Could everything he had seen be fruits of his own imagination?

Suddenly he uttered a cry of joy, startling Nadir.

"But there is Mehlika!" he said. "She is real!"

He rose from the chair and shook Nadir's hands.

"Thank you very much, doctor! You saved my life. Goodbye," he said and left.

"Goodbye. I'll send you the bill," said Udayasekaran.

Hayri did not hear him. He was already down the hall.

***

All night he slept like a baby. Of course, there was no nightmare, or dream. When he woke up, he was like a happy child. He stretched with a smile of satisfaction on his face. This afternoon, he would go to see Mehlika.

If the gurgling of his stomach did not remind him that it was breakfast time, he could have spent the morning in bed.

The refrigerator was almost empty. Since the departure of his mother, he had not been to the supermarket. He was left with the only solution: the great American invention, McDonald's.

He was about to exit his apartment when the phone rang in the living room. He returned to pick it up. I was the sweet voice of the Secretary of Madam Consul.

“Hello Hayri Bey. We were worried about you. Are you all right?”

“I'm fine. Why?”

“We have been waiting you in office, today.”

Damn! This was Monday. Where was his mind?

He tried to explain that the man they had crushed had died. He had to take care of his girlfriend etc. He also had some business to take care of today and would come tomorrow.

“No problem,” said the secretary. “I will inform Madam Consul. Goodbye.”

“Goodbye,” said Hayri, hanging up.

He left his apartment and walked down the stairs without waiting for the elevator.

Outside, a beautiful sunny day was waiting for him. Happy, he started to walk hopping like a sparrow.

The BlackBerry rang to ruin this joyous moment. This was Sinan Bey.

"Hello mon cher. I heard you did not go to work, today. I just want to know if you're okay."

"I've never been better," said Hayri. "Stop worrying for me please!"

"Okay, I understand. I am going to a Turkish restaurant with some friends tonight. Will you come and dine with us?"

"Sorry. I have other commitments."

"Good. I hope it is not with a dangerous woman?"

"I have an appointment with the most dangerous woman in the world," said Hayri.

He hung up the phone and put it in his pocket. A few steps later, he took it out and dialed Madam Consul's office number.

This has been Madam Consul who answered the call. But where's the secretary? Maybe it was better this way.

"Hello madame. I have something important to tell you."

"Ah, Hayri Bey? Something good, I hope."

"I quit!"

"May I ask why?"

Her voice was astonishingly calm.

"I do not know. I want to change my life. I want to do crazy things."

"Such as?" she asked in an ironic voice.

"I want to go to America."

“To America? But why?”

“As I've already said. I want to change my life and America is the land of opportunity, isn’t it?”

She remained silent for a few moments before continuing to talk, still with calm but ironic tone:

“I understand. But be careful Hayri Bey. America is no longer the land of opportunities but opportunists.”

“Thanks for the tip,” said Hayri, to cut the conversation short.

They said goodbye and hung up at the same time.

Hayri stopped walking and remained thoughtful for a moment. In less than a second, he had burned everything. Would he regret later for what he just did?

He looked around to see where he was. He was on the Pont Neuf. “Despite its name it is the oldest bridge in Paris,” he told himself. He leaned over to look at the Seine flowing foolishly below. He took the BlackBerry from his pocket and threw it into the river, checking first that there was no barge passing. Now he was free for real.

A group of elderly women approached him. One of them was holding a map of Paris.

“I am American,” she said.

She did not need to specify. It was almost written on her as a subtitle.

“Do you speak English?” she asked.

“I guess, I do,” said Hayri.

They wanted to go to Notre Dame. It was easy, they were close. He showed them the arrow to the Cathedral and told them the most appropriate platform for the views of approach. The American ladies thanked this 'French' gentleman enthusiastically. One of them even ventured to say 'merci beaucoup'.

He walked to the Pompidou Centre. His stomach rumbled again. But there was no McDonald's in sight. He had to pick one of the cafés. He chose one and entered.

At this early hour of the morning, the café was a rather full of tourists. Everyone was looking at the big screen of a noisy TV. He approached the counter to ask for a croque-monsieur and a coffee. The boss did not hear. His eyes were like frozen on the TV screen. What could there be so interesting?

Curious about what was happening, Hayri tried to concentrate on television. It was the news. Another bomb had exploded somewhere in the world. A video taken on site was showing the site. There were bodies and blood everywhere. He thought he heard a few words in Turkish and pricked up his ears even more. Due to the chatter of customers, it was hard to hear. Yet he managed to distinguish a few key words clearly:

"Attack in Istanbul ... a car bomb .... killing the British consul .... "

One of the tourists shouted:

"Terrorists! They killed the British Consul."

Finally, there was a moment of silence and Hayri could hear clearly:

"Mr. Roger Short, the British Consul-General, who was killed today in an attack in Istanbul. Mr. Short, 59, married with children, was based in Istanbul since..."

The heart of Hayri stopped for a moment. He thought he would faint. With his hands on the counter, he tried to keep his balance. A buzz invaded his ears. He had a terrible desire to escape that place. He walked towards the exit in panic, pushing people.

Once in the street, he felt tears coming. He had never cried since the death of his father, not even for his daughter Seray.

With wet face, he began to run wildly, hustling people out of his way. His tears were limiting his vision. He did not know where to run. He did not know why he was running.

Charlotte, the young girl driving the Mercedes, had her license just two days ago. And this morning, with the help of her mother, she had finally managed to convince her father to borrow the car.

An accident can happen quickly. When she saw a man in front of the car, it was already too late. She did not even have time to brake and hit the man. She was well above the speed limit. The man flew into the air before crashing to the pavement.

It is said that people see 'things' during the passage from this world to the other. For his part, this is what Hayri saw:

While everything was plunging in the dark, he heard the voice of a woman constantly repeating:

"Oh! Please monsieur, please! Do not die!"

He also heard the alarm of a car, then the police sirens and ambulance, but saw nothing of all these.

'It's weird," he said. "I don't feel any pain. It's a shame that I can't go to see Mehlika today."

Suddenly the light flashed around as if there has been a silent explosion; and he could see again.

But he found himself in a totally different setting!

He was among people; thousands, hundreds of thousands; men and women of all races; surrounded by a huge circle of the Venn diagram.

They were walking, rather flowing like the waters of a river. Horrible screams were tearing the ears.

Hayri looked forward to see where this where this 'forced walk' was going. Recognizing the great Gate of Hell in the distance, he thought of Rodin. The master sculptor had well imagined.

Ah, intellectuals! They are always the same, even when dying. What would the art of Rodin do in this Apocalypse?

Surprise! There was no flame in sight. The Gate of Hell, opening onto a large black hole, was swallowing all human beings trapped in this huge circle.

He made vain efforts to escape the crowd but failed. Was he still dreaming? Was that a nightmare or a hypnosis session? Or rather, the hallucinations of a schizophrenic, since from the beginning?

Suddenly, he felt a warm touch to his hand. Startled, he turned to see who was touching him.

This was a little girl who had taken his hand into hers.

“Seray!” he cried with joy.

“Come with me daddy,” said the little girl, by pulling him out of the human flood.

They walked away together.

Then, all plunged back into total darkness of coma.

----- o -----

www.ingramcontent.com/pod-product-compliance
Lightning Source LLC
Chambersburg PA
CBHW030819310726
48980CB00006B/552/J

* 9 7 8 0 5 7 8 1 8 8 1 7 1 *